Three of Swords
By Joanna K. Moore

Triskelion Publishing
15327 W. Becker Lane
Surprise, AZ 85379

First printing by Triskelion Publishing
First print on January 2007
ISBN: 1-60186-032-3
ISBN 13: 9781601860323

Cover design Triskelion Publishing.

"Restauranteur Selene MacPherson, divorced mother of two, sister of one and the town's "fortune teller" (a title that makes her cringe every time she hears it), is on her way to the Old Bedford Days Fair. The portent of doom hanging over her head from the tarot card that keeps coming up is weighing on her mind, and she can't imagine from which direction the danger will come...but whatever is going to happen can't be that bad, can it?

Chief Adrian Burke, newly arrived from Chicago, is Fort Bedford's new chief of police. He's no fan of the charlatans who practice tarot, but he's got a job to do, and intends to do it. When a brutal murder and mutilation occurs, he's at once angered by the small-town incompetence he witnesses and surprised to find such a crime committed in this backwater place. When he steers his investigation toward Selene's sister Izzy, he puts himself on a collision course with Selene's mama-bear instincts. To top it all off, he's oddly intrigued by Selene, by her "knowing" of his past and other things she's simply shouldn't have a clue about. And then another murder occurs...and another...

Ms. Moore accurately and masterfully tells this tale of danger, darkness and death. Selene's psychic abilities play a huge role here, and *Three of Swords* will keep you guessing with its maze of a plot. Adrian is my favorite kind of hero – tall, dark, handsome, tortured by his past – and you'll love watching these two spar and circle each other. The villain is pure, unadulterated evil, and the psychic energy swirling in this tale will have you on the edge of your chair. You'll want to be there when the tension screams up to a fever pitch in *Three of Swords* and a blast from the past hits you right between the eyes! Five Angels and a Recommended Read!!!" **Fallen Angel Reviews**

"Enter a world where good and evil fight for dominance, where magic lives and hope survives, Three of Swords takes you on a ride through terror and mayhem until the truth is revealed. Three of Swords was a story I really enjoyed reading because it had everything, danger, turmoil, magic and also romance. Selene and Adrian were two of the central characters in this book but the secondary characters certainly had a part to play throughout this book too. Ms. Moore has penned a tale that provides twists and turns while also enthralling the reader into perusing its pages and characters that are special in their own way. So go out and get your copy of Three of Swords because it will captivate you just as it did me." **Ecataromance**

Dedication

To my Great-Grandmother, Augusta Knibbe Gerfers, and stories told in the afternoon. This one's for you, Mimmy.

With love to Scott, Brandon, Christine, all my family and friends, and with gratitude to my fellow SARAs. Where would I be without all of you

Chapter One

Three of Swords.
Sorrow. Despair. Loss.

I stared at the card in my hand for a moment, then shoved it back into the tarot deck. I'd drawn the same unwelcome image three days in a row. A strong sense of premonition swept over me, like a tingling sensation in the spine just before an accident occurs on the highway. It was my habit to draw a daily card, to obtain some understanding of the current energies at play. The Three of Swords, with its red heart pierced by triple daggers against a backdrop of dark, stormy clouds, forecast only bad news.

There'd been little shortage of that lately. My entire week had been a long series of disputes and problems. I'd hoped to have some fun tonight, to relax and enjoy myself, to simply be Selene MacPherson, partygoer. This card, however, suggested otherwise. I wondered what else I was going to have to handle before the day was out.

I tucked the tarot deck into the black velvet pouch tied at my waist and took one last look in the mirror. I shook my head at my reflection. I'd put off getting dressed until the last minute. It showed. My long brown hair hung in unruly mounds of curls around my face and shoulders. I looked like Chewbacca from Star Wars. I grabbed a brush and attempted a rescue mission.

My outfit didn't fare much better. The green Irish dance dress fit too tight across the bosom, but it would have to do. It was the only thing I owned that could pass as a costume for the festivities at the Old Fort Bedford Days Fair. The Fair could never be compared to Mardi Gras, but it was the high point of the year for our little beach town, tucked away in the southwestern corner of the Florida Panhandle.

The Festival Committee requested me as the designated fortuneteller tonight. I'd agreed, even though the term fortuneteller rubbed against my grain. I'm called the "town witch", with amusement by some and contempt by others. It was a life-long tag I'd found hard to shake, thanks to my family's rather eccentric reputation.

I'd worked relentlessly to turn the town's focus toward my community work and restaurant business instead of my infamy as one of the MacPhersons. That's why I wasn't so sure it was wise to consent to this Festival appearance. I generally gave tarot readings only to family and close friends, but the Foundation Committee talked me into it, dangling coveted membership in the local Chamber of Commerce as a prize. I'd bitten the carrot.

I finally twisted my hair into a loose chignon, then glanced at my watch. We were way behind schedule. I opened my bedroom door and called out to my youngest daughter. "Lissa? Where are you? Sarabeth will be here any minute."

I grabbed my purse from the doorknob and struggled once more with the bodice of my gown. Too much cleavage. Not an appropriate appearance for a respectable mother of two daughters. Three, if you counted my younger sister, Izzy. I'd raised her since she was young. She still lived in the family home, in the same room she'd occupied since birth.

I'd shared my room once, with my ex-husband. That was another story.

I leaned over the banister of the upstairs landing and searched for my oldest child. "Stephanie! Stop putting on makeup. We have to leave."

"Mama, look what I found. Can I wear it?"

I turned my gaze to the bottom of the stairs. Lissa stood with an old straw hat, bedecked with sunflowers and daisies, perched on her head. It had once belonged to my late mother. It was far too big for her ten-year-old frame, but I didn't have the heart to tell her no.

"Sure you can, baby girl. Where's your Aunt Izzy?"

"Here, and I'm going. Sean's waiting for me out front." Izzy slammed the door of her room, then rushed behind me, her stiletto heels clicking on the hallway floor.

She stopped and gave me a wet kiss on the cheek. "Bye, Big Sis. Have fun at the festival." She ran down the stairs, her frilly black cocktail waitress uniform flouncing around her thighs.

"Izzy."

She turned and glanced at me from the staircase. "What? Frank will fire my ass if I'm late for work."

"Just be careful, all right? I drew the Three of Swords again."

Izzy smiled, then waved at me as she continued her dash. "Oh, sweetie, you know I don't put much stock in divination. Stop worrying and live a little."

Her response didn't surprise me. She'd never taken much interest in exercising the family gift. Her talent for precognitive dreams did little good, since she rarely made the effort to recall her nighttime journeys. As for not worrying, she didn't have to pay the property taxes, feed a household of four, or keep the air conditioners running during the endless, scorching Southern summers.

It was already flaming hot and only early June. I fanned myself with my hand as a trickle of sweat slipped between my breasts. The heat was almost tangible, along with the wet-towel-in-your-face humidity. My costume bunched beneath my arms, sticking to my skin. Izzy opened the front door and rushed to her current boyfriend as he sat astride his motorcycle. The rumble of the pipes on his Harley as he revved the engine only exacerbated my unease. She cuddled behind him and planted a kiss on his neck, then pulled a silver helmet over her long red hair.

"Be careful anyway," I called out. The front porch door banged shut. Maybe I did worry too much. I drew a deep breath and tamped down my concern. Yet I knew I couldn't completely relax. The air held a portent of caution in its breath. What harm could there be in applying a little extra vigilance?

Steph came into view beneath me, giving her sister a playful shove. Lissa turned on her, frowning. "Cut that out," I warned. Steph looked up at me in surprise. Even from this distance, I could see the neon purple eye shadow she'd applied. I sighed, sorry that it was too late for a face washing.

Steph grinned, turning her angelic, sweeter–than–sugar persona to full wattage. I knew immediately she wanted something. "Mom, can Jamie go to the festival with us? Her Mom said she could go as long as Sarabeth watched us."

"You should have asked me before you asked her Mo—oh, all right, yes. Are you two ready?" Sarabeth pulled into the driveway and honked the horn twice, propelling me into action. "Let's go."

I hurried down the stairs and grabbed the front door keys from the foyer table. The girls darted outside, waving at Sarabeth. I closed the door, struggling with my purse as I jiggled the ancient lock. I thought again about the tarot card, the image of the punctured red heart niggling at my brain. Sarabeth honked the horn again, scattering my thoughts. *Let it go, Selene. You'll manage whatever it foretells later. How bad can it be?*

I should have known better.

*****

"Look Mama, funnel cakes. Can we have one, please, please?" Lissa hopped up and down in anticipation, her long brown curls bouncing beneath the oversized straw hat.

Funnel cakes, fried pastries covered in powdered sugar, were Lissa's favorite treat. As much as I tried to steer the girls away from such artery-clogging delicacies, I gave Lissa five dollars and sent them and Steph's friend, Jamie, to the stand to purchase one. Maybe I'd be able to snag a piece for myself, before they completely demolished it.

"They'll be good and wired now, with all that sugar." Sarabeth's plump belly shook with laughter. "Thanks a lot."

"I'm sorry, Sara B. I didn't think about that."

Sarabeth patted my arm and shook her head. "I'm just teasing you, *ma petite*. I'm used to children.

After all, I helped raise you."

I grinned and nodded my agreement. Sarabeth became a part of our family from the moment she'd shown up on the doorstep of MacPherson House, fresh from Louisiana with her wise woman ways and sharp mind, ready to take on the job as Mama's housekeeper.

Lissa and the other girls ran back, the funnel cake already half-devoured on their return trip. Sarabeth and I each grabbed a corner of the haphazard cake and pulled, tearing off a little piece of sugared heaven. I popped it into my mouth and reveled in the experience as it melted into instant cholesterol. I decided I didn't care. It was Festival night. Time to party. I spied Eleanor Reynolds from the Foundation waving at me. Time to work, too. "Gotta go. You girls mind Sarabeth, and don't get into any trouble. You hear?"

"Okay, Mama." Lissa's rosy pink lips sported a white powdered halo. She looked like one of those milk commercials.

Steph paused long enough in her conversation with Jamie to shake her head in the affirmative. Her smooth blonde hair glinted in the afternoon sun, reminding me of her father.

I drew Sarabeth to the side as the girls returned to their funnel cake. "I didn't want to say anything and spoil their good time, but the energies aren't positive tonight. In a crowd situation like this, anything can happen."

Sarabeth glanced in the girls' direction, then back at me. "Don't you worry, *cherie*. I'll keep an extra eye and a firm leash on them."

I hugged her tight. "I know you will."

I hurried to Eleanor and greeted her, then took a seat at my booth. I took a moment to calm down, to still my thoughts. Taking three deep breaths to center my mind and spirit, I removed the cards from their pouch and held them in my hands. I asked help to aid those who came to me, for clear vision and a true heart. When peace settled over me, I lifted my head and waited.

Within moments, a man I'd never seen walked slowly toward the booth. He was tall and long-limbed, about a foot taller than my five-foot two-inch frame. He wore his thick black hair combed back, but the first few strands refused to be controlled. They fell over his forehead in defiance. His looks weren't the type I'd usually give a second glance. I preferred blonde, medium-built men. Yet something about him drew my attention. He stirred me, like a shaft of bright sunlight through a window. Intense, potent, powerful.

I shivered in response and looked away. I wanted no part of that. There was enough intensity in my life already. I broke the odd connection with the stranger and scanned the crowd, taking note of the various people. Many of my frequent customers from the *M & M*, Steph's favorite nickname for our restaurant, *Mimosas and Magnolias*, were there.

One of my regulars, Mr. Swann, strolled through the crowd, his hands clasped behind his back. A rather quiet man in his forties on vacation from up north, he'd been particularly nice to me. He wasn't too hard on the eyes, either. Definitely Robert Redford Revisited. I admired him only from a distance. I hadn't had a date with anyone except my ex-husband since I was fourteen. The whole man-woman mating ritual was a mystery to me, and not one I particularly wanted to figure out.

The fairground already milled with festival attendees. The colorful flowers and streamers, foot-pounding country music and laughter in the air lifted my spirits. I waved at a few of the locals as their children urged them toward the Monster Caterpillar ride. I smiled, glad that I wouldn't have to ride the mechanical bug this year.

A shadow cast over me and I looked up, just as the sun set behind a man standing at my booth.

"Excuse me." A deep, male voice filled my senses. "Do you have a permit to perform fortune telling?"

I squinted up at him, moving to my left to get a better view. It was Mr. Tall and Dark. "Yes, I do. Who are you, and why do you ask?"

"Adrian Burke. Police Chief of Fort Bedford."

So, this was the new guy in town, direct from Chicago. I hadn't met the new Chief yet. He'd been on the job for about three weeks. Local residents were already choosing sides as to whether or not they liked him. So far, the voting ran about fifty-fifty. I wasn't sure where I fell in the polls, but the frown on his face wasn't helping his cause. "Welcome to Fort Bedford, Chief. Here's my permit."

I opened my pouch and pulled out the paper. The law requiring permits for "fortune telling" originated decades ago with my Grandmother, one of the many failed attempts on the part of the town council to curtail her herbal and magical work for her clients. Granny had thrived on the conflict, the battle to uphold the ancient ways. I was the complete opposite.

Chief Burke took the paper from my hands and scanned it, his dark brows pulled low over his eyes. Did this man ever laugh? I didn't see much evidence of it. He returned it to me, a bit of frustration in his expression.

I couldn't resist. "What's the matter? Sorry you can't run me in?"

He cleared his throat as a guilty look crossed his face. "I'm checking to make sure all booths have their proper licenses."

"Really? How many booths have you checked?"

"Just yours, so far."

I picked up the cards and shuffled, but kept my gaze on him. "I see. How interesting. I take it you're not a supporter of Tarot?"

He gave me a slight grin. "I wouldn't say that. Although it does make me think of that Jamaican lady on those old late-night commercials."

I laughed. "Please don't compare me to her. I bet she couldn't get a permit in Fort Bedford to save her life."

I lowered my gaze from the Chief for a moment and pulled a random card from the deck. The Lovers card leapt into my hand, its naked and nubile male and female side-by-side, unashamed and passionate. By the gods, no. I shoved the image back into the stack and set the cards aside. "I'm Selene MacPherson." I put out my hand in greeting. "I own Mimosas and Magnolias. It's a restaurant down on the shoreline."

He took my hand. His grasp was warm and firm, with a confidence that communicated this was no "small town guy". His fingers held the calluses of a man who knew how to work hard. The burn scars on the back of his hand surprised me. He abruptly ended the handshake as soon as my gaze touched them.

I looked up in surprise, a vortex of energy pulling at the edge of my consciousness. The Festival scene around him began to narrow and recede as his image grew sharper. It was as if his spirit demanded my awareness. Against my active will, a part of me pushed open to receive him. A great surge of sorrow rushed forward, like an ocean wave at high tide. The force of it shook me. I'd never felt that much emotion from someone so quickly. It was-

The high-pitched voice of Gladys Miller shook me out of my trance. "I'm praying for you, Selene MacPherson."

Oh, no. Just what I'd feared. Why had I let the Foundation talk me into running this booth? I swallowed my embarrassment and smiled at her. "Bless you, too, Mrs. Miller."

The older woman's mouth snapped shut into a thin little line. She stalked away toward the town gazebo.

The Chief motioned toward her retreating back with his thumb. "A fan of yours, I take it?"

I sat back in my chair and sighed. "No. The Millers haven't liked us since our Grandmothers were girls. Let's just say our ways don't mesh with theirs."

"And what is your way?"

I looked at him, wondering how far I should push

the conversation. I was generally very cautious how much I told others, particularly strangers. "Let's just say my family is known for being tied to the old ways of our ancestors. How about you, Chief? Burke's an Irish name. I bet you were an altar boy when you were young."

Chief Burke leaned a shoulder against one of the white picket pillars of my booth. The breeze blew a thick strand of black hair into his eyes. The sudden urge to reach out and smooth it back unnerved me. Where had that come from? I folded my palms together, containing the impulse.

"Not quite. My father was Catholic, my mom was Jewish. They didn't practice. I'm not much of anything."

Something in his demeanor moved me. "On the contrary. I'd say you're quite a lot."

I bit my tongue in reaction. Why had I said that? His presence confused me. The steady stream of emotions flowing from him was like standing under a waterfall, unable to catch a breath. I was usually empathic to a degree. With this man, it was as if I couldn't stop.

He stood up, straightening his shoulders. The energy around him suddenly shifted, like the sting from a frigid gust of wind. I blinked my eyes a couple of times in reaction as he looked down at me.

"So, is this how it works?"

"How what works?"

He gave my booth a quick, dismissing glance. "The fortune-telling racket. You seem to be the type to make people talk about themselves without realizing it. Is that how you find out what they want to hear?"

I entwined my fingers together and held back a sigh. So much for my empathic skills, I'd failed to pick up the depth of his skepticism. A little ball of irritation circled in my stomach. "No, Chief. It's not a con or a trick. I have a permit. It's been nice meeting you. If you'll excuse me, I'd better get to work so the donations for the Foundation can start rolling in."

I picked up the cards again, diverting my attention. Even with my gaze on the deck, I could sense his affront at my showing him the door. An apology rose to my lips, but I held it back. He'd started it, with his "what they want to hear" comment. I waited impatiently for him to move on. I needed to focus on the positive, to counteract what might be brewing on the horizon.

He nodded in a brisk, military fashion. "Carry on." Then he turned and walked in the direction of the Monster Caterpillar ride.

I shuffled the deck and forced myself to calm. So much for my vote on the new lawman in town. He'd done everything but openly call me a fraud. Being Chief didn't give him carte blanche to be a jerk.

A small voice in the back of my mind nudged me to reconsider my anger. He'd been more surprised than me when that tidbit of personal information popped out of his mouth. I lowered my chin, willing to admit the possibility. I risked a glance in his direction. He seemed no worse for wear. The Chief stood across the walkway, talking with the ride operator. Good. If anyone needed their permits checked, it was probably the owner of that rusty insect on wheels. I smiled as the cards flipped through my fingers.   The familiar feel of the well-worn deck restored me.

I leaned forward on the red cloth covering my table and resumed waving to the partygoers. Eventually a line formed, natives and tourists alike, curious to find out if they had any hope of marriage or if their careers would take off in the future. I could only tell them what the energies indicated in the present.   It was up to them to make their lives happen. A few of my M & M customers were the first to get in line. The handsome Mr. Swann came by to greet me, but he refused a reading.

"No, thanks." Mr. Swann gifted me with a flash of a smile. "I already know what's going to happen. It's too late to change."

I shook my head, hoping to encourage him. "It's never too late, for anything." I secretly hoped he'd amend his decision. A peek into his romantic future might be interesting.

He gave a shy wave as my girls approached, their arms filled with the stuffed animals they'd won. Great, more stuffed animals. Their rooms were already overflowing with down-filled menageries, but the joy on their faces convinced me that we had room for a few extra. They giggled and begged me for more spending money as they stashed their oversized unicorns and giraffes behind my booth. I pulled out a twenty from my wallet and sent them on their way as Sarabeth trailed behind them.

I sighed in contentment as an evening breeze picked up, bringing cool relief from the heat of the day. I leaned back in my chair and gazed at the sky. The moon hung high overhead, bathing the Festival in its glow. It was almost full, lacking only a small sliver. I fixed my gaze on it, taking solace and refreshment from its cool presence. I'd always loved the moon, the night, the sound of the crickets filling the air. Their singing was an irritant to the tourists, but a welcome, familiar lullaby to me. It wasn't summer in Fort Bedford without them.

Suddenly a faint buzzing sounded inside my head, like a swarm of mosquitoes in flight. The moon's image began to waver like water flowing over a flame. The smooth, white face turned red, the dark, rich scarlet of fresh blood. Three swords impaled it, crimson rivers pouring from the wounds at each point. I blinked my eyes, a hard bite of fear piercing me. I gripped the table with my hands as the ruby blob began to spin wildly.

Then it was gone. Nothing remained but the soft, lunar landscape, undisturbed and serene.

I knew it wasn't my imagination. I'd seen the Three of Swords come to life. I stood up and glanced around the crowd for my daughters, my heart hammering in my chest. I needed to know where they were, what they were doing. Whatever this foretold, it was near.

Chapter Two

"What's the rush, Mom? Is something the matter?"

I ignored Steph's question and silently urged her, her sister, and Sarabeth into the house. We'd dropped Jamie off with her parents as soon as the Festival was over. I closed the door behind me and locked the deadbolt. The reassuring click gave me a sense of relief, and I finally drew a deep breath. I straightened and focused on appearing calm and normal for the girls' benefit, placing an arm around each of them. "No, nothing's the matter. I was just tired and ready to go home. Did you girls have a good time? How was the Monster Bug ride?"

"Caterpillar, Mom," Steph corrected. "It was great. Can we go again tomorrow night? Jamie and I saw some kids from school. Tommy was there, too."

"Tommy, as in, too-good-looking-to-be-true Tommy?"

Steph tried for an indignant look, but it dissolved into giggles. "Mom. Yeah, that one. He bought me a soda."

I smiled, restraining my reaction to a seventeen-year-old high school boy sniffing around my daughter, a recent junior high graduate. I vowed to keep an eye on the situation. "I'm glad you and Jamie had a good time. Let's get these clothes off and get ready for bed. First one undressed gets the hot water."

At that, Steph ran up the stairs, stripping off her blouse in a mad dash to the shower. The ancient water heater on this side of the house only had so much to go around. She who struck first got the hottest bath.

Lissa, however, stood next to me and slipped her hand into mine. She looked up, her dark chocolate eyes serious and questioning. My mother's straw hat sat a bit askew on her head, somehow intensifying the solemnity of her expression. She wasn't buying it.

"Something's the matter. I saw it."

"What did you see, baby girl?"

"I saw the fear colors around you when you came to talk to us. You were scared, Mom. Why were you scared?"

I bent down on one knee and rubbed her shoulders. Unlike Steph, who did her best to ignore her natural psychic ability and usually succeeded, Lissa was more like me. At least, the way I'd been as a child. Once she'd opened to her version of the gift, it never left her. Lissa could see the aura of energy around people, animals, and plants if she was in the proper state of mind, or if it involved a person with whom she had a close connection. I could never hide what I felt from her.

How often I'd wished that wasn't true. I'd wanted to shield her from the pain I'd endured after the divorce. I'd wanted her to believe the pretty words I'd used to explain why Daddy left—that he was no longer in love with Mommy, but he would always love them. Steph believed me and clung to the words like a lifeline, but Lissa knew the truth. "Mama just got a little scared, Lissabelle. You know how frightening the world can be nowadays. It makes me nervous to have y'all away from me in such a big crowd. Do you understand?"

"But Sarabeth was with us. She'd never let anything happen to us."

"I know. I was being silly, wasn't I?" I gave her shoulders a little squeeze and grinned. "Hey, why don't you use the downstairs shower and see if you can race Steph for the hot water? Then we'll have some tea, if you want."

"Okay." Her face brightened a little. "Can I have some of Sarabeth's pralines, too?"

"You might as well. What's a little more sugar at this point? After all that funnel cake, you and your sister won't sleep for a week."

Lissa laughed and pulled my mother's hat from her head, then ran down the hall. I could sense Sarabeth approaching from behind. There was no way I was going to distract her with tea and pralines.

"Tell me what you saw, Selene. And don't deny it. I could always feel when the Sight came over you, even when you were little."

I sighed and turned. Sarabeth stood with her arms crossed, her pink cotton dress taut across her ample bosom. Her dark eyes missed nothing. There was no sense in pretending. "I saw the moon turn to blood. It became the Three of Swords."

"Damn."

Sarabeth's frustrated curse surprised me. I stifled a smile, remembering the woman who'd chased me throughout my high school years with a bar of soap to "wash out the nastiness" from my adolescent, push-the-envelope mouth. But I agreed. This vision definitely invited a profanity.

"You can say that again. I've also drawn the

Three of Swords for my daily card for the last three days."

Sarabeth nodded. "Well, it's better than others. The Three of Swords usually means some kind of separation, sorrow, pain, the end of something, like a relationship. That isn't always bad, depending on what it is."

"I know." I frowned, rubbing the little crease between my eyes with my forefingers. "But the way I saw it...all the blood...it feels dangerous."

We walked into the kitchen. I took the tea out of the refrigerator and poured four glasses, one for each of us. I set the girls' glasses on the counter, then carried mine and Sarabeth's to the table.

I sat across from her and took her hand. "What do you see coming? I'm too frazzled to focus."

She looked at me, her dark brows furrowed as she rubbed her thumb over my palm and sought an answer. Finally she sighed and put her other hand across mine.

"I can't get a good handle on it, *bebe*. Can't see through the fog. I can tell it isn't going to be easy. But you'll come out okay."

I lay my head on the cool table, sighing with fatigue. "I want it to go away, whatever it is. I don't want to deal with it. I've had enough. Haven't I earned a break?"

Sarabeth laughed. "You never get more than you can handle. It's your fault for being able to handle so much."

I lifted my head and glared at her. "Gee, thanks, that really helps."

She laughed again in response. I couldn't help

but join her.

I sat up and took a sip of my tea. Was I overreacting? The Three of Swords usually involved relationship troubles. Even though this was a powerful warning, it couldn't be anything beyond our capacity to deal with as a family. I nodded, liking the sound of that. "You're right, Sara B. Things will be okay. We've endured worse than this. We'll do it this time, too."

"Now you're talkin'."

The girls arrived, their hair dripping wet. The fronts of their t-shirts were drenched, but they seemed unaware of it.

Sarabeth growled at them. "Look at you girls, drippin' all over the kitchen floor like that. Were you born in a barn? Go dry those heads before you catch your death. I swear."

The girls immediately turned tail and ran to get their towels. I sat back in my chair and stared. "I want you to teach me how to do that. You say jump and they ask how high?"

"You gotta get old like me, *cherie*. Then you'll see the power of age over the young."

"If I've got to get old, I think I'll wait. Only room for one old crone in this house, right?"

Sarabeth gave me a devilish smile. "Damn straight."

I slapped her lightly on the arm, shaking my head at her friskiness. Another sip of the cold, soothing tea seemed to flow through me and calm my jangled nerves. Everything was going to be all right. Maybe all this meant was that someone was going to face the end of a romance. Most likely Izzy, since she was the only one in the house with a boyfriend. Unless we counted Tommy, and I didn't want to count him. He was too old for Steph, and it was no secret what seventeen-year-old boys wanted from pretty, easily swayed, fourteen-year-old girls. Besides...

The phone rang, breaking my train of thought. Probably a good thing. I was getting ready to engage in a major Mom worry fest. *Positive energy, positive energy.* I rose from the table and snatched the receiver from the black wall phone. "Hello?"

"Selene?" The voice on the line trembled.

"Izzy? Is that you? What's the matter?" A cold shiver ran through me, like the touch of an icy finger down my back. I gripped the receiver tight.

"I need you to come get me. I'm at work, and I need you to come. It's bad, real bad, and I..."

Izzy's voice broke, dissolving into a sob.

I sensed Sarabeth's presence behind me. She'd known something was wrong, the moment the phone rang.

"It's...it's Sean. Come and get me, please? Right now? The cops are here, I have to go, please come right away."

"I will. I'm leaving now. Are you okay? What happened? What..."

The line went dead. She must have hung up the phone or been cut off. I turned to Sarabeth, but she only put up a hand and tossed the car keys in my direction.

"Go to Izzy. I'll stay with the girls."

"I love you." I kissed her on the cheek, grabbed my purse, and ran out the side door toward my Toyota.

The flashing lights of police cars blinded me as I pulled in front of Casey's Oceanside Sports Bar. Our town's entire police force numbered about ten officers. All ten were clearly in attendance, by the look of things. Everyone wanted a piece of whatever had happened.

It made sense. The last real excitement we'd had crime-wise was a year ago, an armed robbery at the gas station on IH10 at the far outskirts of town, one traveler robbing another. High drama for our boys in blue, who usually spent their days breaking up domestic spats between spouses, answering calls for loose dogs in someone's flower garden, or handling petty theft claims from visitors. Not exactly the things upon which you'd base a television action series.

I parked the car at the convenience store next to the Bar and walked toward the crowd at the rear of the business. I craned my neck, searching for Izzy. Where was she? Was she hurt? My heartbeat pulsed faster as I angled my way through the crush of onlookers.

A man towered over the other officers gathered around him. I recognized that dark head of hair. Chief Burke was here and obviously in charge. He gestured this way and that as a few of the men scattered to follow his orders. I pushed my way between two Festival partygoers, ignoring their drunken comments about my costume.

"What do you mean we don't have crime scene tape?" Chief Burke's question carried over the muffled roar of the voices around me.

Another man answered. I recognized him and

the man beside him. I'd known Harlan Roberts and Jake Carlisle since childhood. They'd been my ex-husband's best friends. They'd been my friends, too, before the divorce.

"Well, we ran out of it a while back," Harlan explained, wiping his balding brow with a blue bandana handkerchief. "We just sorta figured we didn't need to hurry on reordering. Nothing ever happens around here. Much. Until now, that is."

"Hey. I got a rope in my truck." Jake leaned toward Chief Burke and Harlan. "We could string it up around the trees here and use that." He grinned, his teeth white against his perpetually sun-tanned face.

"A rope," Chief Burke repeated. "We're going to seal off a murder investigation with a rope. Good God, what were you people thinking when you..."

"Murder?" I pushed forward, all pretense of politeness gone. "Izzy," I screamed, a fine-edged sense of panic slicing into me. "Where are you?" I elbowed my way around a couple of heavy-set women when I lost my footing and stumbled, right into the arms of the Chief.

"Izzy," I yelled again, pulling at the Chief's restraining hold.

"Hang on. You can't go charging into a crime scene. Men, secure this area. Now!"

The men scurried as Jake took off toward his truck.

The Chief tightened his grip on my arms, enough to get my attention. "Stop struggling. Who's this Izzy?"

I looked up at him, a sensation of vertigo washing

over me. "Let me go. I'm here to find my sister. She called and told me to come get her. Where is she? I need to find her."

"Calm down. We'll find her. Sgt. Roberts, do you know this woman's sister?" The tone of the Chief's voice snapped Harlan to attention.

"Yes, sir. That's Izzy MacPherson. She's inside." Harlan glanced at me, his expression softening. "She's okay, Selene."

My knees felt as if they'd turned to water, but I struggled to keep steady. "Take me to her."

"This way." Harlan pointed to the side entrance of the bar. He eyed my costume and lifted his wiry eyebrows in response, but said nothing.

"Are you sure you're all right?" Chief Burke bent down to look into my eyes.

I noticed at that moment that his were a soft shade of baby blue, like the color of the sky on a cloudless day. His expression was completely calm and in control. A sense of safety emanated from him, like safe harbor in a storm. I connected with that energy and took a deep breath, then nodded. Only at that point did he release me.

I walked shakily behind Harlan into the darkened bar. The smell of stale cigarettes, liquor, and a nauseating, discordant mix of men's cologne and women's perfume wafted in the air. I suddenly wished I'd taken the time to eat something at the Festival beside the one bite of funnel cake. My stomach heaved upward, but I pushed it down by force of will.

Finally, I saw her. Izzy, surrounded by men. But this time all the men were in uniform, and it was clearly in an official capacity. Her face streaked with tears, she wrung a spent tissue in her hands as she talked to one of the officers. The relief that flooded me at the sight of her, unharmed and whole, almost sent me into a faint.

She looked in my direction, then dropped the tissue on the floor and rushed toward me. She threw her arms around me, her cocktail waitress uniform flipping up in the back like an old-fashioned crinoline.

"I'm so glad you're here." She hadn't hugged me with this much emotion since our parents died, when she was eleven and I was twenty.

I wrapped my arms around her, holding her close.

"It's Sean. He's dead. They found him behind the bar. He was stabbed. And then he...whoever did it...they...oh God, it was horrible..."

Izzy began to sob. I motioned for the officers to move away until she'd calmed down. They walked a few feet to our right, talking among themselves. I drew Izzy to the nearest table and deposited her in one of the chairs. Grabbing some napkins, I pushed them into her hands and looked for the bar owner, Frank. He was surrounded by police, so I patted Izzy's hand and walked behind the bar to pull her a glass of water.

She drank, hiccupping once or twice between swallows. When she'd finally quieted, one of the officers approached her again.

"I only have a few more questions, Izzy, I mean, Miss MacPherson."

I recognized the young man. Johnny Marshall, a local boy who'd graduated a year after Izzy at the local high school. Izzy looked up at him, her red-rimmed eyes wide and trusting. He smiled at her, then seemed to flush a bit under his collar. The Izzy Effect. No man was safe from it.

"When was the last time you saw Sean Nelson?"

Izzy dabbed her eyes with the rolled up napkins. "Right before I started my shift at seven. He said he'd see me later, when I got off work. He always came to follow me home, to make sure I was safe, that no one...that no one hurt me..." Izzy began to sob again.

My heart squeezed tight enough to shatter. The Three of Swords, in stark depiction. Why did it have to wound the people I loved?

"I understand," Johnny continued. "Did he mention anything to you, anything at all, of an unusual nature? Did he mention a strange situation, an odd encounter?"

"No. He said he'd had a good day at work. He was looking forward to seeing me. He said he had a surprise for me. I don't know what it was. I...now I'll never know." Izzy's voice broke, but she struggled to hold together. "Other than that, he was the same. Happy, joking. Just like always."

"Thank you. If you remember anything else, contact us at the station. We may question you further at a later date. You still live at MacPherson House?"

Izzy looked at the report Johnny handed her. "Yes. Can I...can we go now? My sister, she's here."

Johnny glanced at me and nodded. I reached over and took Izzy's hand. It was cold and clammy. She was in the early stages of shock. I knew it was best that we get her home as soon as possible.

Sarabeth and I could help her in the traditional way.

"Certainly. I'm sorry for your loss, Izzy."

"Thank you." Her voice was barely audible.

I watched Johnny walk away, then stop to confer with some of the other local police.

"C'mon." I lifted her to her feet. "Let's get you home."

She was limp as a rag doll, and allowed me to lead her out of the bar and into the car without a single word. I buckled the seatbelt around her, caressing her hair as she closed her eyes and laid her head on the seat.

"Thank you, Sellie."

I smiled, tears choking at the back of my throat. She hadn't called me Sellie since before our parents died. Sellie was her baby name for me. I could still see her, running behind me on fat little legs, begging me to play with her. I'd thought of myself as too old to play "baby games". After all, I was a big, almost grown twelve-year-old and she was only three, but she inevitably talked me into it, every time.

I closed the car door, then looked back toward the crowd of police. Chief Burke stared at me, his hand stopped in midair in the midst of signing some papers. I didn't know why, but I felt the urge to go to him. I made sure Izzy was locked safely in the car, then I walked back to the bar. He signed the papers and turned toward me as I approached.

"Thank you. You were very kind to my sister and me. I won't forget it."

"No problem. I'm just glad she's all right. Are you taking her home?"

"Yes. She's been through a shock, but we'll be

able to help her."

He smiled slightly. "More of those old family ways?"

"Absolutely." I looked toward the bright lights that lit the area behind Jake's makeshift crime scene rope. Poor Sean lay on the ground, his face shoveled into the dirt of the parking lot. They'd drawn a line around his body, just like in the movies. I shivered in response. I wondered if his life force was still in the area, dazed by all the activity. I prayed for his spirit to find its way into the west, into the Otherworld. It was then that I saw something else.

His hands were stretched slightly over his head, as if he'd tried to catch himself when he'd fallen. His fingers were deathly white and still.

All eight of them.

Two were missing. The pinky and ring finger on his left hand had been sliced off, leaving a pool of blood on the patch of gray asphalt beneath his palm. I looked up at Chief Burke, my mouth open to speak, but I couldn't force any sounds from my throat.

He nodded, glancing at Sean and then back at me. "He was stabbed in the back three times and two fingers sliced off and apparently taken by the assailant. If you or your sister know any information about the victim, anything at all, that might help us, please let us know."

"We will. We'll do whatever we can to help." I stared at Sean, disbelief filling my head. "Something like this has never happened here. Never."

The Chief nodded as his gaze followed mine. "I've seen a lot on the job, but in Chicago. I didn't expect it in a town like this."

I turned toward him. His gaze was cool and impassive, but I heard the hint of something else in his voice. An edginess that belied his calm. It didn't matter now. Not with Sean's lifeless body a few feet away.

"Like I said, Chief. Welcome to Fort Bedford."

Chapter Three

Izzy barely came out of her shock-induced daze long enough to stumble into the house. Sarabeth wanted to give her one of her herbal remedies, but in the end, we realized sleep was probably the best healing agent nature could provide. We tucked her into bed with a lavender sachet beneath her pillow to calm her dreams. Then I turned in for the night.

I put off telling the girls, at least until morning. My parents passed away before they were born. This would be their first experience with the death of someone they knew. I wasn't sure how they would take it.

When the alarm rang at four-thirty the next morning, I was so tired I could barely recall my own name, but within minutes, I was at my regular post in the restaurant kitchen, mixing pancake and waffle batter. I would have preferred to close the restaurant for the day, to give myself time to recover and help Izzy though the aftermath, but the stack of bills in the back office made this a seven-days-a-week business. I couldn't afford to shut the doors. Sometimes I wondered if the business owned me, instead of the other way around.

Five years ago, not long after my ex-husband, Jason, left, I'd renovated the west wing of MacPherson House and launched Mimosas and Magnolias. We're usually greeted by a handful of customers waiting at the door every morning at six am. Life begins dark and early in this part of the Florida Panhandle. I like to think of Fort Bedford as the last stop of serenity before travelers venture into what the rest of the state has become. We're more Mobile than Miami, more genteel than jet set. Life here is leisurely, relaxed, and tranquil.

At least until last night.

I did my best to push from my mind the image of Sean's lifeblood flowing out on the pavement beneath him. I silently said a prayer for him to find his way to the Otherworld and have peace. The image of his hand, with the two fingers missing...somehow that was even worse, more macabre. Was his death a part of the vision I'd seen? Why had the warning come to me and not Izzy? Was there more to this than just Sean's murder? I picked up a bowl of batter and began stirring, needing something repetitive to console me.

"Are you okay, sweetie?"

I looked up at my best friend, Janell, and nodded. "I will be. It was awful, seeing Sean like that. I won't ever forget it. I can't believe it happened."

Janelle shook her head as she separated the bacon for frying. Her short blonde ringlets curled into her eyes, causing her to blink. She blew them away with a puff of breath. They came right back. "I know, it's so sad. Sean's parents used to shop in my Dad's grocery store. They were good people. He wasn't much to speak of as far as ambition. Motorcycles and good times, that was Sean, but he was really nice."

"I hope that's what people will say about me when I pass on," I mused, my mood turning bleaker.

Janelle laughed. "Don't worry, they'll say that. They'll say, 'You know, she was a really nice lady...for a witch.'"

I couldn't help but laugh, mostly because I knew what she said was true. "Yeah, well, they'll say the same thing about you. Good Ol' Janell Wilson. She was an awfully nice lady, for a..." I bit my lower lip, searching for the perfect word.

"For an oddball." Janell laughed even louder. "I like that. I want that engraved on my tombstone. Here lies The Oddball. Get ready, heaven, here she comes."

I shook my head, thanking the Universe for Janell. Even now, she knew how to pull me out of the gray fog encircling me and make me see things in her topsy-turvy way. A way that guaranteed I didn't take myself too seriously. She'd volunteered earlier in the week to come by and help cook for the customers, performing her in-a-pinch chef duties that had literally "saved my bacon" on more than one occasion, but she'd also announced she had a business proposal for me. I dreaded the thought. I ducked my head and focused on my work, hoping she'd forget to bring up her plan. Surely she'd realize after the kind of ordeal I'd endured, business talk was the last thing I wanted to discuss.

It was not a day for such hopes.

"I hope this isn't a bad time, what with Izzy and Sean and all, but I did want to talk to you about my new idea." Janell picked up the Virginia ham and placed it on the slicer. "I had the most fantastic inspiration that will make both of us scads of money."

I sighed, resigned to the conversation. Her eccentric reputation belied a keen, one-track mind when it came to getting what she wanted. There was no sense fighting the tide. "Scads, huh? Go on."

"You know the part of the West Wing you haven't renovated yet? I'd love to rent it from you and open a shop. I'd call it Southern Skies Art Studio. I'd feature my paintings, take portrait appointments, present the quilts and the craft projects I've done over the years. You know I have enough work in my house to fill a whole store right now. I'd pay you rent, and even undertake the renovation of the room. I've checked out the zoning stuff and spoken with the licensing guys downtown, and I've already had a meeting with Roger Harris at the bank. He says I'm a shoe-in for a loan. I could even have it today."

"Really?" An automatic advance? I knew first-hand that Fort Bedford State Bank had well-deserved reputation for stinginess. I'd been turned down for a loan more than once.

Janell sliced a few shavings of ham, the whining sound of the machine filling the room. "Well, Roger and I have...an understanding."

Knowing Roger as I did, I set the mixing bowl on the counter with a thud. "What does that mean? I swear to God, if he's giving you this loan on the condition you sleep with him, I'll hex him into next week."

Janell looked at me over her shoulder. "You don't hex, so that would be worthless. No, Roger isn't pressuring me to sleep with him to get the loan. Besides, I have good credit. No, he wants...a favor."

"Like what?" The first thrum of a headache set up military cadence in my right temple.

"He wants me to paint a portrait of him in the nude. You know, like in that movie Titanic? Only he wants to be Kate Winslet."

I must have stared with my mouth hanging open for at least a minute, while she laughed and sliced more ham. Roger Harris. Balding, middle-aged, overweight by at least forty pounds Roger Harris. Spread on a couch for hours, while Janell created his likeness. Was he going to wear that big blue diamond around his neck, too?

"I know. Yuck, huh? He wants to give the painting to his girlfriend as a gift. He thinks it will turn her on. I'll try and make him look better than he really does, for her sake. Anyway, what about my idea? Are you game for this?"

I didn't know what to say. The plan sounded like a gift from paradise for the M & M. It was perfect. Which is why I asked her to give me time to think about it. The last time I thought something was perfect, it packed up after ten years of marriage and took off with his new girlfriend.

Janell nodded, her blonde curls bouncing around her cheeks. "I completely understand. I can bring you all the paperwork from the attorneys and show you everything in detail. It will be strictly business, so we can keep our friendship separate from our agreement. I'll pay the monthly rent to the bank, so you won't have to ask me where the money is."

She grinned, her face flushed and eager. I could tell she was doing her best to make this as easy as possible for me, yet still obtain her goal. "Bring me the paperwork and I'll think it over. Okay? But no guarantees."

"Great. I think it'll be a terrific arrangement for both of us, and we'll be together more often. Won't that be grand?"

I smiled and nodded. Janell meant well, but she had no way of knowing how much a part of me longed to get away, far away, to be by myself. I was rarely alone. With the constant crush of family, friends, and customers under the same roof, there was seldom a moment in the day that I didn't have someone talking, complaining, or advising me. Lately the weariness settled in my bones at night with a nagging, dull ache. I'd burned the candle at both ends. I was about to run out of wick.

No wonder my "three of swords" vision snuck up on me the way it had. I'd made no effort the past few years to exercise my gift, to keep it honed and sharp like the instrument it was. My gift was as rusty and unreliable as the trunk catch of Sarabeths's old Buick. When you least expected it, the trunk flew open and whacked you in the head. I knew what that was like on an astral level, now.

I ceased my litany of grievances long enough to wonder what Granny would say. She'd probably call it a case of extreme self-pity. "You never know how good you have it until it's gone," she used to tell me. She's probably also ask, "What have you to gripe about?" And she'd be right. Sarabeth was irreplaceable and a vital part of both the household and the business. Izzy helped as a lunch-hour waitress with a real gift for dealing with people. Even my girls could be counted on, especially in the summer, to help in the kitchen with little things like filling the ketchup bottles and the salt and pepper shakers. My two main waitresses, Bethany and Tammy, were top-notch. So what if the endless circus of it all got to me at times?

Janell leaned toward me. "Hey, we'd better get this bacon frying."

I came out of my "lost in space" mode and nodded to her, then grabbed a potato and sliced it for the food processor.

Get a grip, Selene. You have hungry mouths to feed.

*****

By seven, the restaurant was near capacity. Tammy and Bethany had their hands full. I strolled from table to table, helping where I could while Janell kept the food coming out the service window. We served buffet-style, featuring sausage, bacon, waffles, pancakes, and the eternal Southern standby, grits.

I was especially proud of Janell's bacon today. It was perfect, crisp enough to break with barely a hint of pressure, but not too overdone. It took a deft hand to "know when" while frying bacon, and Janell had it. Maybe she'd missed her true calling when she'd chosen the artist's route? I smiled at the thought as I heard the front door open.

The chief entered. I immediately sobered as his presence brought back all that had occurred last night. Bethany walked to his side and offered to seat him. He bent low to hear her over the noise of the restaurant, his dark hair falling over his forehead. She smiled as he spoke, a twinkle in her eye. Ah, the new chief had a fan. I wondered if Bethany's approval was enough to sway the local popularity poll in his favor.

I walked to them and gave Bethany's back a little pat. "I'll take care of this one."

She nodded, a little-girl giggle escaping her. Her cheeks flushed pink as she waved to the chief and walked away.

Good grief. She acted like Brad Pitt was in town. I turned toward him and put on my best hostess smile. "Welcome, Chief. Hungry this morning?"

He smiled back, a little half-grin I was starting to recognize as the best he could muster.

"Last time I ate was lunch yesterday. I decided to check out your place. Heard good things about it from the guys at the station."

"We aim to please." I showed him to a small table near the front window. He sat, his tall, long-limbed frame fitting as best as it could into the antique table and chair. Maybe men didn't come quite so big in the Victorian era. I wished that I had another table to seat him, but this was all that was left, except for a couple of tables for parties of six. He didn't seem to mind, however.

"You can order from the menu." I handed him one from the stack in my hands. "Or, you can order the buffet and have a little of everything. If you want something more exotic, I'd order from the menu. Today's specials are Homemade Cream Cheese Crescents and Mama's Apple Pancakes."

"Sounds good. I think I'll have both."

"Both? Are you sure? That's a lot of sweet this early in the morning."

"I think I can handle it." He looked around, giving the room a once-over. "This is quite a place, Mrs. MacPherson. Impressive."

I followed his gaze, taking in the country-style, white and green "Southern Mansion" motif I'd created. His praise felt good. "Thanks. We've worked hard to make it what it is."

"I can see that."

"And it's Ms. MacPherson. I'm divorced."

"No more Mr. MacPherson, huh?"

I shook my head. "The only Mr. MacPherson I've ever known was my father."

He lifted an eyebrow at my answer.

"I mean, in the MacPherson family, all the members, male and female, keep the MacPherson name. My Mother was a MacPherson. My father changed his last name when they married."

"That's a new one."

I grinned. "No, actually, that's an old one. We're matrilineal. My daughters also carry the family name."

He cleared his throat as he scanned the menu. "Speaking of family, how's your sister this morning?"

I hugged the menus to my chest. "She's still asleep. I'll know in a little while, when she wakes up."

"How about you? That was a lot for a civilian to face last night."

I looked down at the floor and took a deep breath before answering. "I'll be all right. It's just...very difficult, you know?"

He nodded, his gaze serious. "I was wondering about Izzy. Is she your only sister?"

"Yes. It's just me, my girls and, of course, Sarabeth. She used to be our housekeeper, but she's more like family. I raised Izzy after our parents died, and..." I forced myself to stop blabbering and shook my head. "I can't seem to stop telling you everything. Looks like the police and tarot card readers have something in common."

He had the good grace to chuckle, after his comment at the Festival. "Maybe so."

"I'd better put in your breakfast order. Coffee?"

"Yes. Black." He handed me the menu, then smiled again, that little crooking of the left side of his mouth that gave a fleeting flash of his straight, white teeth. There was something endearing about it, as if he was embarrassed to let go.

I stood looking at him a little too long. He glanced down at his hands and then back up at me, his expression reflecting his curiosity. That was enough to snap me out of my character study and hustle across the room to get his coffee.

What was wrong with me? Maybe I really did need to get away and recharge my batteries. I never rattled on like that, to anyone. Much less to a man I barely knew.

I dropped off his order with Janell, poured him a cup of coffee, and returned to his table. In the few moments I'd been gone, he'd put back his stern police face. Too bad. For a few minutes, he'd seemed almost human. I set the coffee in front of him and turned to go, but he had other ideas.

"Can you sit for a moment, Ms. MacPherson? I'd like to ask you a few questions about Mr. Nelson."

"Certainly." I pulled out the chair across from him and took a seat. I fit in the furniture much better than he did. He shifted in his chair uncomfortably, leaning forward to rest on his arms. It was like watching an adult sit down at a child's tea party. I pulled my chair closer to the table.

He took a sip of his coffee, then set it on the saucer. "How long has your sister been seeing Mr.

Nelson?"

"I don't know, maybe a few months."

"Was it a serious relationship, in your opinion?"

"As serious as Izzy can get about any man. She's reluctant to commit too quickly to anyone."

He nodded. "I see. Was she dating other men while in a relationship with Mr. Nelson? Was he aware of these other men, to your knowledge?"

"You'd have to ask her." A prickling sensation at the back of my neck forced me to shift in my chair. What was he getting at?

"Were you aware of, or did you personally witness, any kind of disagreement between them? Fights, harsh words, things like that?"

"No, they seemed pretty tranquil and happy the last time I saw them." I crossed my arms on the table and leaned forward. "Why are you asking this? Are you really concerned, or is it something else? Sounds to me like you're looking at Izzy like a suspect. She wouldn't hurt a fly, much less a man she cared for the way she cared for Sean. You saw her last night. You know what I'm saying."

He gave me a sharp look. "Right now everyone is a suspect, until they're ruled out."

I shook my head, my fingers spread on the table. "But you can't mean Izzy! She was at work, isn't that her—what do you call it—alibi? She was in the bar with dozens of people. They all saw her."

The chief cleared his throat, then picked up his cup and peered into the black depths. "Miss MacPherson's whereabouts for the entire evening can't be established. I'm not at liberty to say more."

A shiver of alarm coursed down my back at his

words. This was insanity.

The Chief set his cup aside. "What about other members of the family? The housekeeper, Sarabeth? What about your ex-husband? Did he have any dealings with Mr. Nelson?"

I stood up, narrowing my eyes at the Chief. "For your information, my husband left town five years ago and hasn't been back since. As for the members of this family, we'll cooperate with the police and answer any questions. But we won't put up with being treated like we're brainless. People come to the front door when they want something down here, Chief. They don't sneak around the back and pretend to be friends. You want to talk to Izzy? Contact her. She'll make herself available."

I walked away, my gait calm and collected while inside me, panic rose like a flood tide. My sister, an official suspect. How could anyone suspect Izzy of something so heinous? The worst thing she'd ever done in her life was fall in love with the wrong men. She wasn't capable of murder. Or mutilation, either.

I walked into the kitchen just as Janell whipped up the chief's order. "You want to deliver this personally?" She gave me a conspiratorial wink.

I snorted in response. "Not if he wants to survive the meal." I stopped, startled by what I'd said. Any more comments like that and I was going to move up to number two on his murder suspects dance card.

I rubbed my forehead and closed my eyes for a moment. "I'm sorry. No, send it out with Bethany. He's really her customer."

"Okay." Janell eyed me with a worried stare. I tried not to notice. I didn't want to get into it with her. I just wanted...what?

I wanted my life back, the way it was before last night. I regretted all the times I'd complained, even to myself. Things could always be worse. Like now, for instance. This was much worse.

The swinging door to the family side of the house opened. Izzy walked in, dressed in old jeans ripped at the knees and a yellow t-shirt. She looked like ten miles of bad road.

"I'll be right back." I was speaking to Janell as I took Izzy's elbow and led her back into the east wing. I didn't want Chief Burke to see her and launch into fresh round of questions. Not yet.

"What's the matter?" Izzy pulled her arm from my grasp. She sounded as if she'd been drinking, her voice whiskey deep and slurred.

That was nothing new. She sounded like that every morning when she woke up. Yet I knew Chief Burke could make all kinds of things out of it, if he heard her now.

The pit of my stomach went hollow as I began to see my family the way the chief might. None of us would look normal. Our family reputation alone would make anyone view us as weird and suspicious, particularly people who didn't know us personally. People such as the chief, who'd been in town less than a month and met us for the first time last night. Under less than usual circumstances. What would he think if I told him my vision? I'd probably find myself locked up for observation.

"Just come with me." I put a hand to Izzy's back and guided her into the living room. She came along, shuffling her feet as if part of her brain was comatose.

She flopped on the couch, looking so much like a rebellious teenager that a spark of anger fired in me. What was going to happen? How was this going to affect all of us, especially the kids? Why had she ever got involved with Sean, for God's sake, and why...?

Izzy closed her eyes as two shining tears slid down the curve of each cheek. My anger immediately dissolved. I sat down next to her and drew her into my arms as she began to sob. She cried for a long time as she released everything she'd endured last night. I held her, patting her back as I'd done since she was little. Her hands clenched and unclenched in her lap. I noticed the dried blood still under her nails. Sean's blood. Had she tried to save him? Had she held him when he died, or was he already gone when they'd found his body? There would be time to go into all of that later. For now, I simply embraced her, for as long as she needed.

Finally her tears subsided. I handed her a cloth napkin from the kitchen that I'd tucked into my jeans pocket. She dabbed at her eyes, sitting up straight.

I turned my body toward her on the couch. "Are you okay? I need you to listen to me. It's important."

"I'm all right." She twisted the napkin in her hands.

"I brought you in here because the chief is sitting in the restaurant. He wants to ask you questions—about you, Sean, your relationship, where you were last night. He's looking at everyone as a potential suspect. Do you understand what I mean when I say everyone?"

I waited until the light came on behind her eyes.

"Oh...God. You mean they think I might have

done it?"

"They think everyone in town might have done it, at this point. I told him to call and arrange a time to speak to you. I need you to pull yourself together. I know it's hard. But this is serious and you need to be ready. I think we should call Mr. McCarty before you talk to the chief."

"Daddy's old law partner? You really think I need that? Oh, God. I didn't kill Sean, Sellie. I swear I didn't!"

I cupped her cheeks in my hands and forced her to look at me. "You listen to me, okay? I know you didn't do it. Don't think for a second that any of us assume you did. We're with you, all the way. Do you hear me?"

Izzy nodded, blinking her eyes rapidly. "Yes, I...I'm going to call Mr. McCarty right now. Get his advice."

"Good. In the meantime, I'll run interference with the chief until you're ready. Okay?"

"Okay." Izzy pulled herself from the couch and climbed the main staircase back to her room, her fingers white against the oak railing.

I watched her as I rested my elbows on my knees, my hands dangling limp between them. I had no idea who could have killed Sean. The idea of anyone in this town being capable of that kind of violence was unimaginable. But the town was changing, along with the world. New people, new opportunities, new ways of life had begun to alter the landscape. Fort Bedford had staggered into the twenty-first century, even though a sizeable number of the residents still fought against the current.

Our local police force, however, remained solidly secure in the "good old days". I tried to imagine Harlan and Jake with this kind of responsibility on their hands. Talk about a joke. Chief Burke was an odd one, enigmatic and distant. I knew nothing about him, or why he'd left a big city like Chicago and moved to comparably tiny Fort Bedford. Wasn't that a bit strange? Sounded like a demotion. Maybe he'd been a pitiful excuse for a cop in the big time and this was all that he could find. That would fit the usual pattern of the Fort Bedford PD. As well meaning as they were, Harlan and Jake couldn't get a job at the local Thrifty-Mart. Yet the FBPD took them on. Not exactly proof of good judgment on the department's behalf, in my view.

It hadn't mattered that much before. Who needed someone highly trained to handle petty, minor incidents? But this was murder. And Izzy, and perhaps other people I loved, stood in the department's investigative crosshairs.

I rose from the couch. If the police thought they could conveniently pin this crime on my sister, they'd have to get through me first. If they couldn't find out who did it, I would. There was one thing the Chief didn't know about the Clan MacPherson.

The motto on our family crest reads, "Touch not the cat without a glove."

Chapter Four

"I'm here as a friend of the family." Mr. McCarty's reedy voice revealed his advanced age, but it still held the strength of authority.

I pressed my ear close to the door, hoping no one suddenly opened it and I wound up flat on my face.

"I understand that, sir. Now, Miss MacPherson, tell me what you remember concerning last night."

I could hear Izzy shifting in her chair at the family kitchen table. If she was uncomfortable, it was most likely due to the piercing stare of the Chief, the one he used when he was in full cop mode. I'd seen it this morning. It wasn't a pleasant experience. He'd make a cloistered nun wonder if she'd done something illegal.

"I've already told the police everything I know."

"I understand this is difficult, considering your loss. But please, repeat what you told them. It might help you search your memory for anything you may have missed."

"Okay." Izzy sighed, a sad sound I knew came from her heart. "Sean took me to work. He was in a great mood. He said he had a surprise for me, something I'd really love. I still don't know what it was. I told him I'd see him when my shift ended at midnight. There were lots of people in the bar, with all the tourists in town for the Festival and the big baseball game on the tube. We have one of those giant TVs in the bar, you know? Lots of game fans. I worked my butt off. We all did."

"I see. Were you in the bar all night?"

"Yes. I only took one break for a while, later in the evening."

"Where do you take your breaks?"

"In the back storage room. Some of the other girls hang out in the ladies' room, but I need peace and quiet when I take a break. It helps me recharge before I get back out on the floor. It's not easy being a waitress, despite how it might look."

"Did anyone see you take this break? How long were you gone?"

"I don't know if anyone saw me. I told Frank I was taking my break."

"What time was this?"

"I think it was about eleven o'clock. I was gone for fifteen, maybe twenty minutes. Why?"

"Based on what we currently know, that was approximately the time the murder occurred."

The family kitchen fell silent at that statement. My fingers tightened on the doorjamb as the implication of his words dug into my bones. Izzy was on break when the murder occurred. If no one could back up her whereabouts, she couldn't prove her innocence without a doubt.

"What are you doing?" A voice whispered behind me.

I turned, a finger to my lips.

Sarabeth scowled, then dragged me away from the door into the living room. "I wondered where you went. The Chief will tan your hide if he catches you eavesdropping. Izzy's got Leslie McCarty in there. You know she's safe with him around."

Trust in Mr. McCarty was almost a family legacy, but I was too frightened by the vortex sucking us down to let him handle it. Izzy needed a MacPherson on her side, fighting all the way.

"I need to know what's happening." I reached out and rubbed Sarabeth's shoulders. I knew she was afraid. Her eyes were a dull, bark-colored brown, with violet circles beneath them. She looked as if she hadn't slept. "I'll be careful. But I won't let Izzy be railroaded. Not as long as there's breath in my body."

"I don't want either of you to get hurt." Sarabeth looked up at me. For the first time, I saw her as she really was...an aging woman, time taking her vitality and replacing it with the first touches of frailty. I hugged her close and silently vowed to keep us all safe.

"We won't get hurt, I promise. Listen, I need to take off after the restaurant closes at two. Can you hold down the fort for me until I get back?"

Sarabeth wiped her eyes with the corner of her apron, then lifted her chin. "Of course I can. You go off for a while, *cherie*, that's what you need. This has been a lot for you to deal with. Relax a bit, maybe walk on the beach?"

I nodded, going along with her assumption. The beach, however, was the last place I intended to visit. I had another location in mind.

The scene of the crime.

*****

The afternoon sun filtered through the leaves, casting a dappled light on the back parking lot of Oceanside Bar. Jake's "crime scene rope" remained strung around the trees. A note barring people from entry flapped in the breeze, stuck to the rope with silver duct tape.

Classy.

I looked around, careful to make sure I was alone. Thankfully, the bar owner decided to close until the shock of the murder died down. Since this town hadn't seen a murder since the late nineteen-fifties, that would definitely take more than a weekend.

I listened, trying to pick up any indication that people were present. All I could hear was the distant sound of the surf and the calls of a few white seabirds overhead. I lifted the rope and crawled inside the area, my palms damp with nervousness. What was I doing? I should go home and forget about this, but the image in my mind of Izzy behind bars for even a moment pushed my feet into action.

I walked toward the darkened bloodstains on the pavement. The white chalk silhouette of Sean's body was still visible on the asphalt, although smeared a bit by the removal of his remains. I knelt beside the area, trying to push back my emotions so my other senses could work. It wasn't easy.

I closed my eyes and took a deep breath through my nose, then blew it out softly through my lips. Three times I did this, to center myself and begin the opening of the gift.

I opened my eyes, observing the area around me with full attention. The gray gravel pavement. The dark blood stains, one where Sean had bled out from the knife wounds in his back, the other where his fingers had been removed. The shadow of the bar's roof as the sun moved toward the west. The smell of the heated parking lot assailed my senses, mixed with the tang of dried blood and the salt of the sea air. The heat of the afternoon and the humidity that always came with it, like a tag-along child that wouldn't go home, seared through my cotton shirt, deepening my awareness of where I was in that moment.

I closed my eyes and took another breath, then moved to the next level of consciousness. I opened myself to what I felt around me, the energies present. I could sense my isolation, but beyond that...what lingered? The muscles in my forehead tightened as I pushed myself further open. I could discern...confusion. Anger. Surprise. Sean's, or the killer's? I pressed closer with my feelings. There it was. It was...a sense of triumph. As if something long awaited had been accomplished. An almost evil glee attached to it, a strange sort of joy. I pulled back, the touch of that emotion like slime dripping off rotting fish. I could smell the scent of it, a hot, tangy, repulsive odor. I couldn't take it anymore. But I'd come close enough to move into the third level. The Unseen.

I took a deep breath and moved into the seeing that takes place without physical eyes, the seeing that comes from the inner eye of the soul. I tried to close out the sun, squeezing my eyes shut as tightly as I could. I don't always have to do that in order to see a vision, but this time I needed every part of my concentration. Suddenly the afternoon daylight faded and I dropped into total darkness.

I strained to see in the inky black. A mist hovered at the edge of my sight, shrouding what I wanted to know. I moved through it until I saw a light in the distance. As I drew closer, I realized it was a security light, the kind found at the back of businesses to ward off burglars. In the little circle of light cast beneath it, a man stood alone. He took a cigarette from his pocket and pulled out a book of matches. He struck a match and lifted it and his cigarette to his face. In the glow from the match, I saw him. Sean.

I moved closer, trying to connect with him, but he seemed unaware of my presence. I knew the teachings of my ancestors about time. Time is a spiral, not linear. It can be touched by those who know how, at any level. It can be bent and extended and expanded, but the past cannot be changed. I edged closer to Sean. At least I could perhaps gain some clue that might help bring his spirit some justice.

He blew out a small stream of smoke, then looked up at the night sky, a smile spreading on his lips. He reached into his pants pocket and pulled out a small blue box. Popping it open, he grinned as he lifted it up to the light. I moved to the left, so I could see the box's contents.

It was a diamond engagement ring. The little white stone sparkled in the security light, shooting off tiny rays of brilliance. It was a modest stone, but obviously heartfelt. The expression on his face was a picture of happiness. He was going to ask Izzy to marry him.

I almost pulled away at that point, the enormity of what both he and Izzy had lost in the twinkling of an eye overwhelming me. He put the ring back in his pocket and took another drag on the cigarette, looking down at his feet as if deep in thought.

Suddenly his head jerked up and he looked behind him, his shaggy black hair swinging over his forehead. He frowned, cocking his head as if listening intently. I looked in the direction he did, but I saw only darkness. He turned back toward the bar, then threw down his cigarette and stubbed it out with the toe of his cowboy boot. He headed toward the back door, about ten feet away. I moved to follow.

It went dark. The security light blinked out, transforming the entire area into a shadowy, moonlit scene. He looked up at the light, scratching the short goatee on his chin thoughtfully.

Suddenly the impact of a knife stab struck his body. He fell to the ground hard, his hands reaching out to catch himself, but the force of the blow was too strong. I moved closer to see, but I couldn't get near him. A powerful, sinister force hovered over him, a shadow with substance. It seemed to swim before my eyes, a sea of muddy, dark colors that flowed sickeningly from one side to another and back again.

I sensed this force surrounded something that was human. I could see the hands of the figure as it drove the knife into Sean's back again and again. It rose over him, looking down with a sense of eerie fulfillment. I watched as the thing took a tool from its pocket and bent over Sean's hand.

I reared back, the strength of the evil repelling me from the scene. I struggled to stay, but I couldn't hold onto the vision. The images slipped away from me like a receding tide. I cried out Sean's name, but nothing happened. He was gone. The fiend who'd dealt his death had his satisfaction.

I came out of the vision hard, my breath in short, raspy gasps, my clothes wet and stuck to my body. I'd fallen on my side, my arms flung over my head and my hair coated with a dusting of dirt and sand. My ears rung loudly, as if I'd been too close to a power generator operating at full blast.

I looked up to see the Chief bent over me, his hands on his knees and his eyes dark with anger.

"What the hell do you think you're doing?" he snarled.

I was in deep trouble. I pushed myself onto my elbows and risked another glance at him. Not a good idea. He looked as if an aneurism lay only seconds away. A little vein throbbed in his forehead. The tips of his ears turned bright red. Oh, yeah. He was about to blow, and I was the target.

I went on the offense. "I'm doing what I have to do. Are you going to help me up, or what?"

The Chief stood, his eyebrows jerking skyward. He looked to his right, as if at a loss for words, then reached down and took my hand, hauling me upright with one pull.

"Damn it. I ought to run you in right now for crossing the police line. Such as it is."

"I know I'm not supposed to be here, but I..."

"Damn right you're not supposed to be here! What is it with you, MacPherson? You don't seem like a stupid woman."

I glanced at him sharply but refused to rise to his bait. "I'll ignore that. Let's face it. You suspect my sister of murder. Jake and Harlan can hardly find their way out of a paper bag, and they're your top officers. Put yourself in my place. What would you do, if it was your sister? Just sit back and hope they don't screw it up, hope that their blunders don't send Izzy to prison for a crime she didn't commit?" I poked a finger at his chest, my emotions getting the better of me. "C'mon, let's hear it. What would you do?"

His lips thinned as he listened, his breath released in a long sigh. He slung his thumbs in the belt loops of his jeans and looked down at the pavement. Finally he turned his gaze to me and spoke.

"If Harlan and Jake were my only hope, I'd think I was screwed. But I'm heading this investigation, not them. Your concern doesn't excuse your breaking the law. This area has been cleared, but it's still an investigation site until it's released. You could have destroyed some remaining evidence that might put your sister in the clear or finger the real killer. Did you think about that before you crossed the line?"

"If I crossed the line, it was precisely because I was after that kind of evidence. The kind that only I...," I paused, realizing that I was about to say too much.

"Only what?"

I took a deep breath, knowing that what I was about to say could open another can of worms for his fishing expedition. But he was going to hear about me eventually, from someone in town, maybe even from Harlan or Jake.

"The kind of evidence that only I can obtain."

"And what kind of evidence is that? You aren't a trained professional. What could you possibly contribute?"

"Spiritual evidence."

He crossed his arms at that, looking down at me with a renewed frown of frustration.

"Spiritual evidence. What, you gonna talk to the

victim's ghost or something?"

I swallowed, looking away from him before answering. "If his ghost allows me to contact it."

"You're nuts, aren't you? It doesn't stop with just tarot cards. What are you saying, that you're some kind of psychic?"

I looked up at him, the tone of his voice stiffening my backbone. "Yes, I am."

He snorted a short laugh, then turned and lifted the rope for me to walk under it. He followed me, dusting off his hands on the legs of his jeans.

"Go home. And stay there. I don't have time for this. Be grateful I'm letting you off."

He walked away from me toward his black Ford truck parked at the front of the bar. I watched him, wondering what I should do. I followed my instincts and called after him.

"What about the engagement ring?"

He stopped in his tracks, then turned his head slightly to the left. "What about it?"

"The engagement ring that Sean had in his pocket. I saw it in my vision. I saw the cigarette he was smoking. He put it out just before he was killed."

The Chief turned toward me even more, giving me a side view of his body. He dropped his chin and looked at me, his eyes narrowed. "How did you know about the cigarette? Or the ring? Did Sean tell you?"

"No. I didn't know about the ring until I saw it in my vision. That must have been what he wanted to talk to Izzy about after work. I saw him killed, Chief Burke. I can tell you what happened."

"How could you know these things? Has you

sister divulged this information to you? Are you covering for her?"

A surge of alarm fired in me. I was making matters worse. "No. You've talked to her. Did she know anything more she did last night?"

"No. Her story was exactly the same. But..."

"She won't be able to tell you anything more, because she doesn't know anything more. She didn't do it. I saw the murder. That's why you found me on the ground the way you did. I was having a vision. It's...part of my gift."

He rubbed his forehead, as if a dizzy spell had come over him. That was probably close to the truth. I knew this was a lot for him to take in, but I had no choice. I had to make him listen. I needed to tell him the vision, in detail, to see if what I saw jived with the evidence. So much was riding on this. I prayed quickly that he wouldn't reject me or take this as a ploy to protect Izzy.

I walked to the Chief's side and put my hand on his arm. He looked down at me, his eyes full of doubt and suspicion. I understood both emotions. "I know this sounds strange. You live in a world where things like this don't happen. Your world is full of facts, provable data, and only what you can see and touch. But there's more to the Universe than that. My gifts are a part of it. I need you to listen to me. I need to tell you the things I saw. You're the trained professional here. Help me, and let me help you."

He stared away for a moment or two. I could sense the wheels in his head turning as he struggled to put together what he'd known as truth with the new reality I'd shown him.

He faced me at last and looked into my eyes. Tension and frustration rippled in his energy like static electricity. "I don't understand any of this. It's crazy. But you know things that no one else but the investigative officers know. I can't ignore that, even if I want to."

I released my held breath. "Then what do you want to do?"

"Go back to your house. It's time we put all the cards on the table, and I don't mean tarot."

"Unless that might prove helpful, you mean?"

"Good grief," he murmured, as he led me to my car.

Chapter Five

Sarabeth gave a surprised look when I walked into the family kitchen with Chief Burke behind me. He was probably the last person she expected to see twice in one day, particularly in the family side of the house. We generally never let strangers into what we saw as our private sanctuary. But the events of last night had changed the rules.

"Afternoon, Chief." Sarabeth wiped her hands on a dishtowel. "Would you like some tea?"

I couldn't help but smile. Despite her misgivings about the Chief's intentions, Southern proprieties must be observed. She'd raised me the same way. We'd offer a fire-breathing, two-headed ogre a cool drink and the best seat in the house, just to be neighborly. Not that the Chief reminded me of one of those. At least not at the moment.

"Thanks." The Chief stuck his hands in his jeans pockets as he scanned the kitchen. "I'm starting to develop a taste for the cold stuff."

"You won't fit in around here until you do." Sarabeth slung the dishtowel over her shoulder and walked to the refrigerator to retrieve the tea, her dark blue house slippers shuffling across the floor.

I sat down at the kitchen table and indicated for the Chief to do the same. He took a seat, his expression inscrutable as he fixed his gaze on me.

I did my best to appear unaffected. I returned his gaze and lifted my chin in a show of self-confidence. *Yeah, that's right, Chief. I'm a cool customer.* Except for the fact that my insides were shaking so hard, the

Inquisition might as well be back in session with me on the rack.

Sarabeth returned with the tea and began to sit with us, but I shook my head ever so slightly, hoping she'd understand.

She did. She patted my shoulder, then turned her back to the chief to give me a warning glance, advising me to be careful. I knew she'd listen at the door as soon as she left, but I didn't mind. It was the Chief I was worried about. He'd already heard enough in the bar parking lot to make this conversation precarious.

Sarabeth paused next to the Chief's chair. "Well, I'm going to check on the girls. Nice seeing you."

"Same here." Chief Burke extended his hand.

Sarabeth took it, closing her eyes slightly as she gazed at him.

Heightened energy rose around us like a shimmering veil. I knew what she was doing. I gave her a frown.

Sarabeth grinned. "Well, I reckon we'll be seeing a lot more of you around here." She gave me a smug look, then waddled out of the kitchen.

I shook my head as she left. Darned old busybody. She needed to stay out of other people's heads unless invited to enter.

The Chief turned to me, his gaze suspicious. "What was that all about?"

"Nothing. Just Sarabeth being herself. She's harmless, I promise."

"Right." He crossed his arms over his chest. "Look, you brought me here to tell me what you think you...saw. So shoot."

"Are you always this pleasant, or is this as good as it gets?"

"You're off the subject." He leaned back in his chair, his expression as stony and cold as the first night I'd met him.

I looked away, put off by his change in attitude. He'd been almost reasonable twenty minutes ago, but now he was firmly back under a cloud of surly derision.

Under any other circumstance, I'd tell him to take a hike. But Izzy was at stake. The killer remained on the loose. My girls, my sister, Sarabeth...they were my responsibility. Now that I'd seen the evil enveloping the killer, how could I sit by and do nothing? What about the danger to the townspeople? Would my grandmother have given up? I knew the answer to that.

I looked back at the Chief and crossed my arms, mirroring his posture. I didn't want to expose my inner life to this man, but there seemed to be no other choice.

I shifted in my seat, turning my body away from him. "My family roots go back to Scotland, Ireland, France, and Wales. For as long as anyone can remember, the MacPhersons have had what the old ones called the Second Sight."

The Chief lifted an eyebrow.

"Clairvoyance, clairaudience, pre-cognitive dreams, visions, empathy."

He stared at me as if I'd grown an extra head during the conversation. I pressed on.

"I receive visions of things that have happened in the past, that are happening now, or that might happen in the future. I can sense the emotions of others. We call it empathic sight."

I paused a moment, unsure how much to say. My natural instinct warned to hide, don't tell, keep silent. But it was too late for that, in light of what had happened.

"Other members of my family have gifts, too, but in different forms. We all have something. I used mine to try to help in this investigation. The question is, are you going to let me?"

The Chief sat silent for a moment, staring at me with such intensity that my stomach began to tighten in apprehension. Finally he pushed away from the table, shaking his head. "What is this? You want publicity for your restaurant or something?" He gave a brief laugh. "I bet you got the information about the ring and the cigarette from Harlan. I must be getting slow." He leaned back in his chair, his face relaxed with what I realized was relief. He thought this was a farce and he was glad. He didn't have to change. He only had to ignore me in order to return his personal universe to order.

"Are you in denial, Chief?"

"Of course not, I'm... Wait." He scowled. "You really believe this stuff, don't you? Does that old lady believe it, too?"

I stood and walked around the side of the table, anger throbbing through my body. "I need you to hear me out concerning the murder. You said you would."

"C'mon. I admit you had me going for a little while, but this? You can't expect me to believe it." He looked up for a moment as if imploring the heavens for help. "If you want to live in fantasy-land, go ahead. I've got an investigation to run."

He rose to leave, pushing his chair out of the way. His shoulder brushed against me as he headed for the door. I stumbled backward, surprised by his sudden movement. He mumbled an apology and reached out with both hands to steady me.

The vision struck the moment he touched me. Blood, night, rain, ice. Searing pain. His pain. Bone-wrenching, nightmare-inducing agony. I could hear his scream as two cars impacted with great force. I smelled the pungent scent of gasoline. Then I saw the flames.

I cried out. He pulled his hands away, taking a couple of steps back.

I could barely speak for a moment. Finally I opened my eyes and looked at him. "Is that how you got the scars on your hand?"

He cradled his hand closer to his body, eyeing me with an almost desperate expression. "What do you mean?"

I could barely speak above a whisper. "The car accident. At night, in the rain. I saw ice on the road. You were hurt. Very badly."

"How do you know that? You got somebody checking up on me?" He moved closer, fury flashing in his eyes. But what I sensed in him wasn't anger.

I steeled myself against his panic and focused on compassion. "I told you. I can see things. I saw the accident. I saw you were seriously injured. I saw..."

"What?" His voice faded into something quieter, darker.

"I saw a woman in the car. She was beautiful.

Pale blonde hair, a dark grey coat with a silver fox collar. She was laughing..."

He sank down into his chair, his head bent forward. "Madelyn."

I crouched down next to him, one hand clutching the edge of the table.

"I bought her that coat for Christmas, right before—the accident." His head hung even lower as his memories pulled him toward a place I sensed he spent the majority of his time avoiding.

I don't know what came over me. I didn't even like the Chief. But I stretched out my hand and caressed the thick black hair at his temple, the way my mother used to do to soothe me. He leaned into my hand for a moment, then lifted his head and looked at me. His cerulean eyes were dark with mourning. I knew what it was like to live in that particular level of hell. No light, no air, no sound. Existing, but not really alive. As soon as I noticed what I was doing, I snatched my hand away.

The Chief didn't seem to notice. He took a deep breath and sat up, his hands on his knees. His energy shifted as he forced his recollections to re-submerge. I wondered how much it took out of him to constantly keep them buried.

He stood, running his hands through his hair. "Look, I recognize what you're trying to do. But this is too much. I need to think. Please, MacPherson, stay home. No more digging into crime scenes. That's an order."

I sighed. His energy had completely receded into the box where he kept it shut tight. I'd lost him. "I hear you." I watched as he walked out the back door.

I sat at the kitchen table and stared through the window, gloom shrouding my spirit. What could I have done differently? I'd failed. Without the Chief to hear me out, the information I'd obtained would go to waste. Possibly at a very high cost.

*****

An hour later, I was elbow-deep in a sink full of sudsy water when I heard a knock at the back door. Wiping my hands on the dishtowel, I opened it.

The Chief stood on the bottom step, his expression still wary, but with a different light in his eyes. "Let's start over. Tell me what you saw about the murder. I'll listen."

I stared at him for a moment, unsure how to respond. "What changed your mind?" I suddenly felt as wary as he. His attitude took quite a change in the space of sixty minutes.

He looked down at his feet, then back at me. "Madelyn. If you knew about her, then maybe you're not out to lunch about this crime. I'm willing to give you a chance, at least."

An underwhelming vote of confidence, but I'd take it. I stepped aside and let him in, then led him to the kitchen table. My wariness kicked up a notch as I sat and faced him. There was something about him that was intimidating, like deep water at night. I knew better than to go swimming where I couldn't see the bottom. I crossed my legs and folded my hands in my lap.

The Chief waited patiently, his previous scowl put aside. This was at least a beginning. I had no idea how long it would last.

I took a deep breath, then fixed my gaze on him. "I saw Sean, standing under the security light..."

                                    *****

By the time I'd finished telling the Chief the details of my vision, he'd filled up several pages of the notebook he carried in his pocket.

"You couldn't see the perpetrator clearly. Why not?"

I sat back in my chair as I considered his question. "I'm not sure. It may mean that whatever evil he's attached to himself literally has a life of its own. It envelops him, drives him. He can't see beyond it. It owns him."

"Great. We've got a killer driven on some kind of supernatural fuel. Tell me anything else you can see."

I closed my eyes and brought the vision to my memory, slowing reviewing it like a video in slow motion. All I could see was the putrid, dark brown ooze that surrounded the killer. That, and..."The hands. I can see the hands."

"What?"

"I can see the hands of the killer. They're the only things I can see clearly. They're masculine. Sort of small and square, not the hands of a big man, not like yours. He's a white man. From the look of the hands, he's not a youth. He's maybe in his thirties or forties."

"Good, don't lose the image. What else?"

I shut my eyes tighter, struggling. "I can see the knife. It's got a black handle. Looks like it's about ten inches long." I frowned as another instrument came into view. "I can see the tool. The tool the killer used to...cut."

"The amputated fingers. What does it look like?"

"It's smaller than I'd expect. It has two handles; it looks like the kind of tool I'd use to cut small branches, but it's shaped differently, sharper and more curved. It looks like the kind of tool you'd cut...cable, or something."

He nodded. "Cable cutters. That makes sense. That may be information we can use to help identify the killer."

I opened my eyes and looked at the Chief. He was writing in his notebook, his dark hair fallen forward. I was glad he was taking my vision seriously, and yet...I was afraid. I was close to this murder, far closer than I'd ever imagined I'd be to an event like this. I feared not only for myself, but for everyone I loved. I shivered and wrapped my arms around my shoulders.

The Chief stopped writing and looked up. "What's wrong?"

"Nothing. I'm fine."

"Nice try. I can see it in your eyes." He stopped writing and leaned in my direction. "Look, I know. You've never been brushed by something like this. You're scared, right? I'd be, if I was in your shoes."

I shook my head. "No, you wouldn't. You're a police officer. You've seen it all."

The Chief nodded. "You bet I have. But I still feel fear. It's the training that keeps the emotions in line and keeps me alive. Let me help you."

I hugged myself a bit tighter. It would be so easy to draw from the strength of another person, to rest in the shade of his concern. But I couldn't let go. If I did, I might never make it back. "I don't like this. I'm afraid for my daughters, my sister, Sarabeth. I want to help, but I don't want the word to get out that I'm doing it. I don't want to draw negativity toward us any more than it already is. I have to take care of them, Chief. They're my responsibility."

"Adrian."

"What?" I looked up at him.

He smiled, an almost three-quarter smile. A lot, for him.

"Adrian. That's my name. Chief is what I get at the station."

I wasn't sure I wanted to be on a first-name basis with the Chief...um, Adrian...but it was rude to refuse him, especially in light of how far he'd been willing to bend in my regard.

I glanced at the clock on the kitchen wall. It was almost six-thirty. The family would be downstairs in a few minutes, eager to have dinner. "Can we finish this another time, Chie... Adrian? It's late. I need to get my household moving."

"Certainly." He stood and gathered his notes. "Let's meet tomorrow morning. How about the M & M?"

"The breakfast rush slows about ten-thirty, then it picks up again at eleven or so for lunch. I really won't have time until after we close at two."

Adrian nodded. "Two-thirty then?"

"Fine," I was suddenly anxious to have him leave. His body filled the kitchen with his presence. His emotions were too intense, too raw, putting me off-kilter. I hadn't yet figured out how to shield myself from their effect.

He turned to leave by the back door when Sarabeth walked into the kitchen. "Where you going, Chief?"

"Heading back to the station."

"You have time for dinner, don't you? Police officers get a dinner break, right?"

Adrian grinned and faced her. "I believe they do."

"Good. Then take a seat and get ready for some of Sarabeth's Famous Fried Chicken." She laughed and gave me a quick wink.

I groaned inwardly. Oh no. The Merry Matchmaker was at it again. She'd trotted a dozen men through this kitchen in the five years since my divorce, hoping to "set a spark". All of them were duds. Not even gunpowder could have set off a reaction. She simply couldn't believe that I had no interest in romance. My ex had taught me about real life. I was still reeling from the lessons.

Adrian was another matter. He wasn't some local guy from the bayfront that Sarabeth dragged home. He was the police chief, currently investigating Izzy under suspicion of murder. What was she thinking?

"I'm sure the Chief has more important things to do." I gave Sarabeth a stern look. "After last night and all." I stressed the words, hoping to get through her thick head the impropriety of her invitation.

"Nonsense." She shook her head, blowing my hopes out of the water. "He's still got to eat. Why not eat where the eatin's good?"

"She's got you there," Adrian leaned against the counter, watching the interplay between Sarabeth and me.

Did he find this amusing? "I don't think it's appropriate for you to eat dinner and socialize with people involved in the investigation." I made sure my tone was blunt. Enough to send him packing.

"I ate breakfast at the M & M this morning. It's about the same. Just a different side of the house."

Sarabeth grinned at him, then pulled out the frying pan.

This was ridiculous.

Izzy and the girls came through the door at that moment. The three of them were initially taken aback by Adrian's presence in the kitchen, but within a few minutes he was sitting with Lissa and listening intently to her opinion concerning why frogs only croak at night.

Steph took surreptitious glances in his direction as she whispered to Sarabeth, who nodded in agreement. The appearance of a strange man in the family side of the house was probably the most disconcerting thing that had happened around here since Lissa's pet garter snake escaped from his cage.

Izzy was the one who surprised me. She sat across from him at the table, talking quietly. My gut instinct screamed to tell her to get away from him, don't speak without your lawyer present, yet whatever he said appeared to comfort her. She brushed her long red hair out of her eyes as she smiled at Lissa, who included her in the very important frog croaking discussion.

How had Adrian's visit suddenly spun out of my control? This was a bad dream in the making, only I wasn't asleep. I glared at Sarabeth, who only smiled at me and returned to humming a tune as she breaded the chicken.

I knew when I was defeated. There was no alternative but to try and endure the evening. I turned to the cabinets and gathered plates, forks, and knives. I usually focused only on the task at hand, working as quickly as possible to accomplish my goal. It was the only way I knew how to function.

Yet tonight held a strange distinction. The touch of the soft cotton of my long skirt aroused me as it brushed against my legs. It was as if I'd never noticed the experience before. Swish, swish. The caress of the material almost drove me mad.

I grew aware of my body in a way I'd never encountered. The weight of my hair on my shoulders, the grazing of my breasts against my blouse as I reached for a set of glasses, the coolness of the breeze on my face as I walked through the kitchen...all of it, exquisite and evocative.

What was the matter with me? I glanced at Adrian, his chin tucked in his hand as Lissa launched into another of her favorite subjects: why sunflowers turn toward the sun. He nodded and grinned that half-grin of his as she giggled. He was certainly a changed man around children. The tension lines around his eyes disappeared. He looked younger, more upbeat. I picked up the plates and started toward the table.

They clattered in my grasp as I froze.

I'd never been like Lissa. I'd rarely, if ever, seen the auras of others. There was one around Adrian. It was a lovely emerald green, with a big ball of clear, deep blue above his head. The green showed he was healing—I assumed from the trauma of the accident—

but the blue over his head indicated that he was in touch with the Higher Power.

That surprised me. He seemed so closed off and shut down, certainly not someone in touch with Spirit. But there it was. I couldn't deny it.

Over his heart area, the green was a murky, dull olive. Instinctively, I knew it had to do with Madelyn. Whatever she'd been to him, her loss wounded him to the core.

He looked at me over Lissa's head and gave a smile. The moment his gaze touched me, the dull olive color over his heart brightened in the middle. A clear, grass green light rose and spiraled in my direction, lifting a few inches away from his body.

I pulled back, stunned. What was that? I faced the counter and straightened the plates, scolding myself for giving in to delusion.

"Mama?"

The high lilt in Lissa's voice caught my attention. I turned toward her, concerned. Her dark eyes wide, she smiled in an embarrassed, awkward way.

"What is it, baby?"

She giggled, her small hand over her mouth. It was then I realized the problem. She'd seen the spiral of light. I hadn't imagined it. She slipped out of her chair and walked toward me, then pulled at my shoulder until I leaned down.

"I think Mr. Burke likes you." Another round of giggles caught her.

"You silly thing." I laughed, letting her know I wasn't angry with her. "Go help your sister with the drinks, right now." She scampered to the other side of the room, still giggling.

I approached the table and handed the plates to Adrian. "Here. Make yourself useful."

"Yes, Ma'am." He took the plates, then gave me that little smile as he set a dish at each chair.

A hot shiver of pleasure shimmied up my spine. I walked away, then opened the refrigerator door and stuck my head inside.

Oh God.

This was the last thing I needed.

Chapter Six

Adrian's cell phone rang just as Sarabeth set the steaming plate of fried chicken in front of him. He took a deep breath of the mouth-watering aroma, his eyes closed in rapture. Then he mumbled an apology and rose from the table to exit into the hallway.

Sarabeth watched him for a moment, then heaved a sigh and sank into her chair. Her usual *joie de vivre* dimmed as she glanced at the heavily laden table. What was wrong? I reached out to place my hand on hers when Adrian returned to the room.

"I'm sorry. I have to leave. Police business."

"But I was going to show you my worm collection," Lissa's bottom lip edged into a pout.

He smiled at her, but the look in his eyes remained distant. "Next time, okay? Selene, may I speak to you for a moment?"

The sound of my first name on his lips took me aback. I wasn't sure he'd remembered it. He seemed to favor calling me MacPherson, up until now. I rose from the table, patting Sarabeth on the shoulder as I passed. I picked up the sadness in her energy field, thick and heavy as molasses. I frowned, then vowed to question her about it as soon as I returned.

Sarabeth lifted her eyes to Adrian, her expression solemn. "Y'all come back now, y'hear, Chief? There'll always be a plate of fried chicken in the refrigerator, as long as I'm doing the cooking."

The tension in Adrian's gaze softened for a moment. "Thanks. I won't forget."

He motioned for me to follow him to the front

door. I walked behind him, noticing how his tall, muscular body seemed to fit within the high-ceilinged rooms of the House, as if he belonged there. Visions of him dressed in tartan and brandishing a claymore danced in my brain before I pushed them away. I shook my head, amazed by my own foolishness.

He opened the front door, then leaned on the frame. I stopped beside him.

"What is it? What's the matter?"

He jerked his head toward me. "Harlan was on the line. Another body's been found. This time near the Festival grounds."

"Oh...no. Who...I mean, what did..."

"There's more. Fingers missing. Sheared off by a sharp instrument. Four of them this time."

"I can't believe this." My ears began to ring as the edges of my vision narrowed. If I didn't sit down, I was going to pass out. I stumbled to the chair next to the window and collapsed into it. Adrian followed and knelt in front of me.

"Come with me to the crime scene."

I pulled away from him, pressing my back into the cushion. "What? No. I don't belong there."

He gripped the armrest next to me. "You're already a part of this, Selene. You wanted to prove yourself to me. Well, you did."

I rose and walked across the room, struggling to take a deep breath. How could he ask this? Wasn't he listening?

I turned and pointed toward the kitchen. "No! Look in that room, Adrian. I have children. Do you think I'd expose myself in public and bring more danger to them? We don't know who the killer is. He could be anyone, anywhere."

I spun away, burrowing my hands in my hair as I pressed hard on my temples. A sense of vortex pulled at my emotions, sucking me toward a dark void. "What do you think would happen? Do you think Gladys Miller is the only one who hates us in this town? I can't get mixed up in this any further. You were right the first time. I'm not a trained professional. I have no business being there."

Adrian followed and spun me to face him. "Look, I don't understand your...gift. A part of me still has doubts. All I know is that you have the ability to access information that we can't. Help us, before this psycho kills again."

I couldn't think. All I could feel was the vortex of darkness filling my brain and Adrian's hands on my skin, holding me firmly in this world. I pushed away, breaking the contact.

The vortex swallowed me.

"No." I wrapped my arms across my chest. "I won't. You can't ask this of me. You don't understand."

Adrian stared at me for a moment, his lips thinned. I could sense his disappointment. His anger at me mixed with a strange sort of sympathy. His fear matched my own, although it sprang from a different source. The sharp, metallic taste of panic rinsed through my mouth. Nausea threatened to shift into a full-fledged bout of sickness.

His head snapped up as he made his decision. "All right. I have to go." I knew he wanted to say more, but he strode away, slamming the door behind him.

I stood in the living room for several minutes, my gaze fixed on the door. He didn't comprehend what I was up against. He didn't know what it was to be hated simply because you were different.

I'd already put the girls through so much, just by being MacPhersons. I'd been loyal to the family, at times to the detriment of what they might have wanted or needed. I'd been a child in this house, in this town. I knew what that life was like. I knew the pain, the embarrassment, the utter desperation to be seen as "normal."

The fear dug deeper, sinking its tentacles into my heart. What had I been thinking all these years? Why had I willingly put my children through this?

I walked to the window and looked out at the fields behind the house. Sea grass, as tall as Lissa, grew wild and free, blowing in the breeze off the Gulf. I clutched the white lace curtain next to me, balling it in my palm.

Why had I stayed here? If I'd left, things might have been different. My girls could have grown up in privacy and peace. Maybe...maybe even Jason wouldn't have abandoned me, if we'd moved far away and started over. My head dropped at the thought, my throat tightening in response.

Now the murders. They were already close, too close. How could I go out there and walk around a crime scene, use my gift in the open, and stir up talk in the town? It would prove every crackpot theory true and create new ones.

I'd struggled so hard to shape my image, to change the image of the family. I'd kept a low profile and learned to fly under the radar of the local busybodies. I'd done what I could to remain loyal to what I'd been taught but still appear "harmless" to onlookers. It had worked for the most part. The modest success of the M and M with the locals showed their rising level of acceptance. But to use The Sight in plain view? That crossed into another realm. It would put me firmly in the "wacko" category for almost every person in town. Worse yet, would my work draw the murderer's notice? Would it put my babies in the line of fire?

Adrian was insane. I'd already done what I could for the town, by giving Adrian the fruits of my vision. I wasn't my grandmother. Her ways weren't even in my capacity. It was time to take care of me and mine. No one else would.

I spun toward the kitchen and pushed the door open. Resolve pulsed through me. That is, until I saw the looks on the faces around the dinner table.

Sarabeth stared at me with the tired, drawn expression of a woman who'd failed. Izzy's huge blue eyes held the look of surprise, as if her idol had fallen from the pedestal. Stephanie's gaze was sullen as she bent over her plate, her fork suspended above a glop of mashed potatoes.

It was Lissa who broke my heart. She looked up at me, her chocolate-brown eyes glistening. "Why, Mama? Why didn't you help Mr. Burke?"

They must have overheard everything. Damn.

I reached down and smoothed Lissa's hair. "I can't help him, baby girl. Not the way he wants. It would put us in too much danger. I have to think about our family first."

Stephanie's gaze shot up at me. "How come we

don't get to decide that? Maybe we don't care about the danger. Maybe we just want to stop the guy who killed Sean."

Izzy began to cry as Stephanie leaned over to embrace her. Lissa began to sniffle as she watched them.

I looked to Sarabeth. "Help me explain it to them. Tell them why I have to do this, why it's the right thing."

She shook her head slightly. "I can't." She turned and refused to look at me.

"Fine!" Tears filled my eyes. "Go ahead, blame me. You're all so good at that. You're on board with me, all the way, as long as I do whatever you want. Well, I'm sick of it. I can't do it all. I can't be it all. Not anymore."

I don't know what came over me at that second. I only knew I had to flee. I turned and threw open the back door. Dusk was falling, casting the sky with a purple-gray tint. The color of mourning. I ran across the field, ignoring the burrs that clutched at my dress like tiny green children begging for my attention. I ran until my lungs tightened, until I could no longer draw a sufficient breath.

I fell at last, my knees hitting soft, wet sand. I'd run blindly in the deepening darkness, my eyes blurred with tears. Somehow I'd come to the one place that held solace for me.

The sea.

I leaned forward on my hands and clutched at the sand, deep sobs racking my chest. I never cried, not when my parents died, not when Jason left and never came back. Not when the burden of all I'd taken on in my life pressed down like a boulder, threatening to crush what was left of the real me. If anything of the real me even existed anymore. My tears mixed with the sea, joining me with my truest Mother.

Finally I fell forward, too exhausted to hold myself upright. I rolled onto my back as a small wave washed ashore, lifting my hair and swirling it around my shoulders like a caress. The sky was dark now, the first star peeking out in the heavens. I shivered from the wet and cold of the sea, but I didn't move. I was clear, empty, and swept clean. I wanted to stay that way. To not feel, not need, not want, ever again. Blissful nothingness. I closed my eyes and took a shaky breath.

"Rise, Selene. Cast the spiral."

I opened my eyes as the whispered voice rang in my ears. It seemed to come from both within and without at the same time. It was a murmur, yet I could hear it distinctly above the roar of the surf. I closed my eyes again, wondering if I'd begun to hallucinate.

"Rise and cast, Selene. The time is short."

This time there was no mistaking it. I sat up, my hair soaked and heavy down my back. I pulled the sodden mass of my skirt from the sand as I struggled to my feet. I faced the ocean as the full moon rose to my left, its shimmering whiteness stark against the black night. Taking three deep breaths, I lifted my arms and sought to join myself with the Power.

"Great Mother, I come before you. By Land, Sea, and Sky, I ask for aid, for help, for connection." I lifted my arms to the stars as I visualized the silver roots of connection flowing from my body, deep into the sand beneath me, far out into the ocean before me. Immediately a surge of life and power began to flow back in return, welcome and joy in its embrace. When the surge filled me to the brim, I turned to the east and extended my right index finger.

"A spiral of protection I cast about me. Wherever I am, may the Mother be." At these words, a single ray of blue-white light shimmered from my fingertip, radiating upon the sand. I turned in a spiral toward the west three times, until surrounded by a triple circle of energy. I raised my arms and the spiral lifted, until I was enclosed within an egg-shaped ball of light. The roar of the waves muted as the ball closed over my head. I was between the worlds, between this world and the world of Spirit. Here was the "thin place", where each can be accessed by the other. I sat down on the sand, only slightly aware that it was growing warm beneath me. I stopped shivering and closed my eyes. The Great Mother of my people was present.

I waited, knowing to remain patient and open. Fears threatened at the edge of my mind, but I let them pass like gusts of wind. I remembered what Granny used to say about fears...to neither give them notice nor struggle against them, only to let go and "be". I was so exhausted in every way, that wasn't difficult. I was a vessel with nothing inside. The void had taken me.

Yet I knew from earliest childhood teachings that nature abhors a vacuum. If one does not fill the void, something else will come along to fill it. It was a choice. I suddenly realized that the Mother had come to offer me such a choice.

I opened my eyes at the thought. Apprehension shook me. I had a strong urge to open the spiral and escape, but I held fast and waited. My fingers clutched at my knees as the compulsion to flee continued to throb through my veins. I focused on breathing—in, out. Anything to still the battle within me.

At last, a deep calm swept over my body. I exhaled with pleasure. The Mother had come. I opened my eyes and saw The Cailleach within the spiral. Her silvery-white owl perched on one bony, gray-cloaked shoulder as she gazed at me with a twinkle in her eye.

"Hail, Great Cailleach." I lifted my hands to honor her.

"You have come far, Granddaughter." Her hands caressed the staff upon which she leaned. "Yet my hearth and cauldron have not seen your presence for many months. You have chosen the world and not me."

I looked down, shamed that I had pushed aside the spiritual in my quest to conquer the corporeal. To be ordinary, successful, respected. I'd worked endlessly to fill my girls with materials blessings, yet I'd allowed their spirits to become underfed. I'd done the same to myself.

"I'm sorry, Grandmother." I folded my hands together. "Now a great danger faces us. I need your protection. I need you to take me and mine into your mountain cave to keep us safe. Please help us."

The Cailleach shook her great white head and sighed. "Still you do not understand, Selene. The cave is the place of initiation, but not of life. You are not called to the cave. You are called to life, and to the service of others. Are you so afraid that your mind has been erased of all that you have learned? This is not to be continued." The Cailleach looked over her left shoulder. "Come, Anna. You will speak to your descendant."

My heart froze when suddenly my grandmother appeared at The Cailleach's side. She stood in the dark blue dress she always wore for prayer and ritual, the long sleeves of the velvet swaying around her slim wrists. She gazed at me, then stood straight and crossed her arms.

I knew that gesture. A lecture was soon to follow. Yet I couldn't quell my joy at the sight of her, even in her discontent.

"Selene Marie MacPherson, you run from a plea for help? You are not a MacPherson if you do. We never run from battle. Touch not the cat without a glove."

I shook my head. "You don't understand. This is murder. The girls, Izzy, Sarabeth, they could all be in danger if I help. I could be in danger. So much could go wrong, so much could happen. I can't risk it. I don't have enough left inside me to endure it. I...oh, Granny, help me." Tears began to slide down my cheek as I closed my eyes.

A soft palm touched my face and drew me out of my pain. Granny was next to me, her faded blue eyes soft and compassionate. I wasn't sure how it was possible, but she had physical form. I could touch her, hear her, smell the sweet, flowery scent of her favorite bath powder. I threw my arms around her and held her. Her familiar, delicate-bird arms, so fragile on the outside and so strong within, embraced and rocked me. It had been an eternity since I'd felt cared for, secure. A little spark of renewed life fired within my spirit.

At that moment, she released me and stood.

"You know what to do, Selene. You have always known what to do. Of all my children, of all my grandchildren, the Mother chose you to lead the Clan with my passing into the Otherworld. You know this, don't you?"

I nodded, my eyes downcast. I didn't want this. I didn't feel qualified. I didn't feel strong enough. But I couldn't deny the truth. I was The MacPherson. I told myself it had no meaning in the modern day. Yet I knew that was a lie. The unspoken had been said and there was no turning back.

Adrian's request for help drifted into my mind. I moved to shut the words out.

"No." The Cailleach drew my attention as my grandmother returned to her side. "Do not shut out the words. Adrian Burke is key to this situation and to your life. If you refuse his presence, you will indeed be in great danger, in more ways than you presently realize. You must allow him to come within the sacred circle of the MacPhersons."

"He barely believes, Great Mother." I rose to my knees. "How can I allow him into the sacred circle? Into what is improbable and crazy to him?"

"You will know," The Cailleach smiled, the expression in her eyes inscrutable. "In the meantime, rise. Return to your home. Prepare yourself and follow through on his request. Do not fear, Selene. The MacPherson has my special protection. Be wise

and cunning, but do not fear. I protect what is mine.
You, your children, your loved ones. Life will not
leave them unless I myself cut the thread. Do you
understand?"

I nodded, my mind clearing and the calm of the
Mother filling my heart. I pulled myself to my feet
and stood with my lifted arms bent at the elbows and
my palms facing out. "I honor you, Great Cailleach,
and I revere you. By Land, Sea, and Sky, and the
Spirit of Flame, I am yours."

She raised her staff, white owl feathers dangling
from the tip. She brought it to touch both my
shoulders, then briefly at my brow. "Be you blessed
and empowered. Be not afraid. Listen, think, and
know. Most of all, trust in what is true, trust in what
is love, even if your human mind states otherwise.
Truth and Love are the greatest powers. Be blessed,
my own."

With that, she and my grandmother faded from
my sight. I stood a while, gathering my strength,
taking inside myself the remainder of the energy still
swirling inside the egg. Then I turned to the east and
extended my index finger once more.

"The spiral is open, but not removed. May what I
do be what the Mother approves." As I turned to the
left three times, the egg-shaped spiral collapsed,
disappearing into the sand with only a twinkling of
light remaining. Finally, it faded completely. The
wind, sound, and fury of the waves returned at full
strength as it whipped the heavy strands of my hair
across my face.

I lifted my burdensome skirt and began to walk
toward the wooden boardwalk. Then I began to run.

Time was short, just as the Great Mother said.

*****

The area near the County Fairgrounds buzzed with uniformed men, police cars, and flashing lights, just as they'd been last night at the bar. Tonight's crowd of onlookers outnumbered yesterday's by three to one. The second night of the Festival had barely begun when the body was discovered, based on the phone call Adrian received. The Foundation must have immediately closed down the festivities. The partygoers remained with nowhere else to go but a macabre side trip to a murder.

I shook my head as I noticed the gaily colored Festival banners flapping in the night breeze. I'd intended to bring the girls here tonight, talk with friends, maybe eat a giant roast turkey leg. Those thoughts seemed to be part of another lifetime, a million miles away.

I'd pinned my hair up into a haphazard chignon and pulled on jeans and a white t-shirt in my haste to get to the site in time. I hadn't even stopped to talk to the children. I only told them I had work to do. They'd nodded to me and joined hands as I ran out the door and jumped into my Toyota.

They knew where I was going. Things had changed now. I didn't want to consider what that might mean. I only knew I had to follow what I had promised.

I saw the back of Adrian's head as I edged near the crime scene. Jake's ubiquitous rope barrier was up again, wrapped around some telephone poles and a tall pine tree. I wondered what he'd use next, once he ran out of cord.

"Adrian," I called out. He didn't hear me. He continued to talk to the officers gathered around him, his hands motioning in different directions. I tried again, almost screaming his name. Still no reaction.

Instinctively, I drew a deep breath and calmed myself, then opened to his energies. I could sense him...the anxiety, the anger, the pain, the pressure to "do it right and not screw up". I pushed through until I saw just a glimmer of the man who had sat at my kitchen table and listened to my daughter with rapt attention. I reached out and touched that part of him as gently as I could, as I whispered his name.

"Adrian..."

He immediately stopped talking, his hands abruptly stalling in mid-air. He slowly turned, his eyes wide. He looked in my direction, his gaze connecting with an intensity that shook me. He turned to the men and said a bit more, then walked to the police line.

He lifted the rope and dragged me under it, then advised the crowd to pull back. One of my steady "coffee and pastry" customers, Bubba Wolcheski, moved into position, backing up Adrian's words with muscle. A couple of partygoers, already deep into their celebration beverages, complained about my entrance into the crime scene. They backed away when Bubba lifted an eyebrow at them. Bubba was not an officer to trifle with. He rarely spoke. His solid bulk usually did all the talking. He nodded to me as Adrian drew me into the darkness, away from the investigation lights.

"What just happened? I could hear you inside my

head. What are you doing here? You said you didn't want to help."

He held my arms so tightly that a twinge of pain shimmied up to my shoulders. I shook him off, then faced him.

"I changed my mind. Damn it, Adrian. I don't want to be here, do you understand? But I am."

He looked at me for a long moment. Finally, he spoke. "How did you do that? How did I hear you inside my head?"

I glanced away, as confused as he. "I don't know. I've never been able to do that with anyone. Only with you." I stopped talking when I realized the truth of what I'd said. What did it mean? I didn't want to go there.

Adrian stared at me, as if gauging my sanity. Or perhaps his. Then he nodded and motioned for me to follow. I walked carefully behind him, trying to step only where he indicated. Even though most of the vital work had been completed by the look of things, I dreaded doing something wrong that would hamper the police efforts to collect evidence. I'd learned more than I'd wanted to know about crime scenes over the past twenty-four hours.

Adrian led me to the body still on the ground. The pool of blood surrounding it smelled sharp and tinny in the humid, June heat. The flies buzzed around our heads, searching for the source. I gagged involuntarily. Adrian handed me his handkerchief, then advised the two officers bent over the body to allow me access.

They looked at Adrian with surprise, then frowned at me as if I was the worst kind of interloper.

I met their gaze, recognizing them as friends of the Millers. Wonderful. The Gladys Miller Fort Bedford Hotline would be burning the telephone wires within the next fifteen minutes. It might move even faster with email.

For a moment I thought to turn back, to refuse, to pretend I wasn't meant to be there. But the picture of my Grandmother's face in my mind stiffened my spine.

I lifted my chin, daring the men to speak. They stood up and backed away, like wary dogs in an alley. *Yeah, that's right, boys. I'm the bigger dog.* At least with Adrian behind me.

I crouched next to the deceased, bending low to peer into his face. Thankfully, I didn't recognize him. He must be a tourist in town for the festivities. At least this made it a bit easier to bear. But not much. A life had been snuffed out, a young man in his prime. He looked about thirty-five, his dark, wavy hair a bit longer than was fashionable. He was in the same position as Sean—on his stomach, knife wounds in the back. I shifted my gaze to his hand, then gagged again when I saw the four fingers missing. Another pool of blood seeped from those wounds, casting the man in a sort of grotesque, crimson figure eight.

"Is it all right if I touch him?" I looked up at Adrian.

Adrian stood over me, his hands on his knees. "Yes. The coroner is almost ready to take him for autopsy."

Autopsy. I didn't want to fill my mind with that image just now. I took another deep breath, centering myself as best I could under the circumstances. I wasn't sure I would be able to see or sense anything. I only knew I was supposed to try.

I put out my hand and gingerly touched the man's elbow. The soft cotton of his shirt stirred me, as memories of childhood inexplicably came to me. I saw a boy, running with other children along a seashore. It looked like Cape Cod, somewhere in the Northeast. Was it the man? Or did it have to do with the killer? I closed my eyes tighter and struggled to move closer.

Suddenly the scene shifted, spinning wildly as if I'd boarded the Caterpillar ride that Steph loved so much. I could see the Festival grounds, smell the scent of the turkey legs and the cotton candy. I realized I was seeing through the eyes of the murder victim. His vision moved side to side, quickly, as if he was searching for someone. I could barely hold onto the vision as all the sounds and colors and smells assailed me. I felt Adrian's hands grasp my shoulders, but he seemed far away, as if in another world.

The man continued to walk up and down the fairgrounds, until finally sighting a woman. He strode to her and caught her by the waist, spinning her around. I heard her laughter, felt her kiss as she threw her arms around him.

"There you are." The woman offered him a piece of her cotton candy. Her grass-green eyes shone with affection as I saw his hand take a piece for himself, then feed some to her. I could feel his sexual attraction for the woman, his urge to take her away and be alone. I squirmed, uncomfortable to be this close to the victim's private life. Yet I knew I had to follow what I saw.

He kissed the woman again, then told her he'd be right back. He walked toward the pine trees surrounding the Fairgrounds. His pulse pounded as he laughed to himself. He was looking for a lover's spot, a place to take the woman and spend a few minutes of quality groping time. His impatience for her, the heavy heat in his groin growing hotter, only fueled his search. He walked deeper into the woods, his gaze again swinging from side to side.

He heard a crack. The sound of a branch snapping. He swung around, expecting that the woman had followed him. I could feel the huge grin on his face as eager expectance surged in him.

It wasn't her. It was a man. I could only see the dark silhouette, walking slowly toward him.

"Hey, man. I'm not trespassing, am I?" The victim relaxed, lifting the beer bottle in his hand to take a drink. He didn't sense the danger.

I did. I tried to warn him, to stop what was coming. Adrian's hands tightened on my shoulders, but he seemed even farther away than before.

The shadowy silhouette of the man moved closer, making no reply. The victim grinned, then offered the mystery man a drink. The flash of a knife flew past my vision to the right. I heard the victim scream. The attacker had missed. That time.

"Help. Help!" the victim cried out, throwing the beer bottle at the attacker as he ran toward the Fairgrounds. I could feel his fear, taste his panic. His heart raced, blood roaring in his ears, while the dulling effect of the beer dragged at his feet.

The attacker caught up with him. This time with deadly accuracy. He plunged the knife into his back with the force of a sledgehammer. The victim screamed as the knife fell three more times. He staggered to the edge of the Fairgrounds and collapsed. His voice, barely audible, gurgled with his last breath.

"Angie..."

I started crying, hovering over him as I lifted away with his soul. Adrian began shaking me, gently at first and then with more strength. I could hear him, feel him, but I was locked in the terrifying vision. I began sobbing uncontrollably. I felt as if I was dying with the man. At last I heard another voice.

"Selene. Come out. Come back, little one."

It was my mother. Her sweet, melodious Southern drawl filled my head with the sound of love and safety. I immediately turned toward it. When I did, I saw Adrian at the edge of my consciousness, his hand stretched out to me. I smiled and took it, wiping away my tears.

Immediately I was out. I was back at the crime scene, on my knees as Adrian held me in his arms. Sweat poured from me, drenching my T-shirt. I looked around, a sense of vertigo spinning the landscape. I couldn't see anything but light. It must have been the bright strobe lights of the investigators. But they couldn't hold a candle to the shocked stares of the onlookers. I'd given them quite a show.

Adrian glanced once at the crowd, then lifted me into his arms and walked away toward the parked patrol cars.

"I'm sorry, Selene," he murmured, his lips against

my forehead. "I had no idea. I didn't know what it did to you. I wasn't sure I was going to get you back. Damn, you scared me."

"Scared me, too." I felt dazed, as if I could see with my physical eyes yet also see from above, an observer outside myself. I looked up, my head falling back and bobbling a little. Adrian opened the door of his truck and lifted me inside, then handed me a bottle of water from behind the seat. He leaned on the doorframe, watching me as I drank and grounded myself into this world again. Finally I looked at him.

"You saw it again, didn't you? You saw the murder." His expression was dark, serious.

His words brought the images back to me, like the shock of a cold bucket of water over my head. "Yes. Send the men into the woods behind the body. That's where the stabbings took place. It started there, not at the Fairgrounds. Go, Adrian. Before something important is lost."

He straightened, the vein in his neck pulsing. He turned to leave, then looked back. "Lock the doors. Don't let anyone in."

I nodded. "Yes, I will. Hurry. I'll...be here when you get back." I didn't know why I said that. I only knew it was true.

He paused another moment and hurried to his men.

I took another drink of water, then leaned back in the seat. My hair was wet and sticky around my face, but I didn't care. I focused on breathing and recapturing my balance.

Slowly, an acute perception of my surroundings crept into my psyche. The hairs on the back of my neck rose, demanding my attention. I sat up, peering into the night. The darkness of the thick pine forest, looming twenty feet high above me, changed from the beloved trees of my youth. They became the hiding place of evil. The abode of a sick, horrid rage. It sought only to feed. It was nowhere near finished. I could sense that truth, as strongly as I could feel my heart pounding in my chest.

I slammed the truck door and frantically locked it. I looked around the cab for a weapon. Adrian's nightstick lay on the floor behind the driver's seat. I lifted it and gripped it in my lap. I was ready to strike out with every ounce of strength in my body. I would do whatever it took to end this malevolent force. It wasn't done with us, or with this town.

A hard shiver crawled up my back and I tightened my hold on the nightstick. I knew one more thing, without a doubt.

It had seen me.

Chapter Seven

At least an hour passed while Adrian and his men searched the woods. I sat in the truck and closed my eyes, using whatever skills I had to determine if the energies of the murderer remained in the area. It was the only help I could offer.

I knew it wasn't enough. When I was younger and worked with my gifts every day, the experience was like swimming through still water. Not anymore. My spiritual muscles were achy and stiff. I felt like an athlete recovering from an injury.

I leaned my head on the seat and sighed. The Cailleach had been right. I'd been focused entirely on the mundane—money, bills, the business. It was understandable. We had to eat. I had to put clothes on my children's backs. But it was more. I'd exhausted myself in the effort to be seen as normal, to earn acceptance in the town for me and my children. I told myself it had all been for them.

But had it? How much of it rooted in the fact that Jason preferred another woman to me, another life to the one we'd shared? How much of it based in the need for someone to tell me I was good enough?

I glanced out the window and rested my elbow on the locked door as I shoved my bedraggled hair out of my eyes. I didn't have time for this. The momentum of what I'd become a part of pulled me along at lightning speed. I needed my wits in place in order to survive, not lost in regret.

A brief flash of light in the darkness caught my eye. I whipped my head around, squinting to see despite the inky black of the woods. A fresh rush of adrenalin throbbed in my temples. I clutched the nightstick with both hands as I scooted lower in the seat. Surprise was a factor I wanted on my side.

The handle on the truck door jiggled. I screamed, the nightstick in front of my face, ready to bash in the head of whoever lurked outside.

It was Adrian. I sighed with relief and flipped open the lock.

He gave me an apologetic grin. "Sorry about that. I didn't mean to scare you."

I noticed the little crow's feet around his eyes, the blue cast of exhaustion in the hollows. He looked terrible. But he was a blessed sight, compared to what I'd been picturing in my mind the past hour. "It's okay. How's it going?"

Adrian glanced back at the crime scene. "You were right about the murder happening in the woods. We found the victim's blood there, a few footprints. But that's all. Whoever this killer is, he's good. It's like he's getting help from the pros."

He crossed his forearm on the top of the open doorway and rested his forehead. He looked so worn and spent; my heart went out to him.

"You know whatever I can do to help, I will."

He looked into my eyes and gave me a tired grin. "Thank you, Selene." Then he glanced away. I could sense his unease with the situation. The city fathers wouldn't make it easy on him, calling in the "town witch" for advice. There would be hell to pay.

Adrian stood, his more formal "police self" slipping into place. "I'm imposing a curfew on the town. We need to keep people off the streets. I'm also ordering the cancellation of the rest of the Festival."

I nodded, knowing that his decision wouldn't be met by many cheers. Adrian was shutting down the biggest source of yearly revenue for the town. His actions wouldn't add to his popularity.

I took a deep breath and loosened my grip on the nightstick. The fact that my fingers hadn't burrowed their prints permanently into the leather surprised me. "Is there anything else you want me to do tonight? The girls and Izzy will be frantic if I don't show up soon."

He shook his head. "We're about done here. If you'll wait, I'll escort you home."

I started to protest, to say that wouldn't be necessary. But something inside me stilled my words. "Thank you. I'd appreciate that."

He nodded, a bit of awkwardness filling the silence between us. I didn't know what to say. Adrian had gone from surly stranger to...I had no idea what. I'd only known him twenty-four hours, and yet the connection between us was palpable. I needed to get away from him, to sort out what stirred between us. It was the logical thing to do.

Which was why what I said next made no sense.

"Would you like to stop by the house? The fried chicken you missed is probably still in the refrigerator."

"I bet it is." A small, tired grin played on his lips. "And I could sure go for some food. You're on. Be back."

"Okay," I heard myself reply. What was the matter with me? I didn't issue invitations like that to a man.

Adrian walked away, his thumbs hooked in the belt loops of his jeans, his black leather jacket tight across his shoulders. The night breeze lifted his dark hair, giving him a mysterious look. For a moment, he seemed less like a man than a sleek, black cat, stalking beneath the low-slung branches of a tree as he surveyed the jungle. I shivered in response and looked away.

I was out of my league.

*****

By the time we arrived home, all the lights in the house were out except the one over the stove. I closed the front door quietly behind Adrian and put a finger to my lips. We crept down the hallway until we reached the swinging door to the family kitchen.

I half expected to see Sarabeth at the old pine table, a cup of steaming coffee to her lips as she waited for her *petite* to return. But she was nowhere to be found. We were alone.

I walked to the refrigerator door and opened it, spying the foil-wrapped plate inside. One chicken leg peeked out from under the aluminum. My mouth watered at the sight.

I looked over my shoulder at Adrian and grinned. "See, I told you. Plenty left."

He nodded, an answering smile on his lips. "Just like Sarabeth said."

He bent over the sink and washed his hands, the scent of the rubber gloves he'd worn at the crime scene filling the air for an instant. He'd removed his jacket, leaving it and his other police paraphernalia in the truck, although his radio and weapon lay on the counter in somber reminder. The soft chambray blue workshirt he wore suited him, giving a gentler look to his lean, muscular physique.

I reached for the soap and began to wash as well. The warm water and the solace of the lavender-scented suds crept into my spirit. I wished the soap could do as good a job on my memory as it did on my fingers. I shivered; the recollection of the impact of the knife on the victim's back rippled through my body. My head spun for a moment. I dropped the soap, watching indifferently as it danced around the drain.

Adrian shut off the tap and looked into my eyes. "You okay? Whoa. Hold on."

I looked up at him, but he seemed to be a bit out of focus. My ears began to ring as my vision of him narrowed. Hmm. This must be what happens when you pass out. Interesting. I heard someone giggle and realized it was I.

Adrian drew me to the kitchen table and sat down, pulling me into his lap. Before I had a moment to protest, he pushed my head between my knees.

"Hey!" I protested, slapping at him with limp fingers. What was he doing? But immediately my head began to clear.

"Just relax and breathe, Selene. You haven't eaten all day, I bet."

My head felt heavy as I hung upside down, my nose brushing the denim of my jeans. "I ate. I think. Maybe at breakfast."

Adrian chuckled. "You get the first bite of chicken. You need it more than I do."

I sat up quickly, and then regretted it. "Ow, my head." I looked at him, lifting my chin as I struggled to hold onto my dignity. "I can take care of myself. In case you haven't noticed, I'm a big girl."

"I've noticed." His hands tightened on my waist. He grinned, trying to appear light-hearted, but it was too late. I saw the flare of something more in his eyes, a look I hadn't seen directed toward me in a very long time.

My instincts screamed to stand up, get out of this strange man's lap and pull myself together. But all I could do was look at him. I was caught in a snare of longing that I didn't understand. Didn't want to understand. Oh, he was so beautiful.

Danger, Selene, a distant voice in my head whispered. It sounded vaguely like Jason. A small shiver of apprehension brought me to my senses.

I latched onto the first excuse I could find in order to escape. "I'll get some plates."

I moved to rise, but Adrian's hands held me firm. "Selene."

The need I heard, the wonder and conflict wrapped around the breath of my name, broke my resistance. I turned and looked into his eyes. His height brought his face level with mine, even though I sat on his lap. The gentle strength of his hands at my waist, the warmth of his breath whispering across my collarbone, it had been so long since I'd been this close to a man. I'd forgotten what it was like to be touched, to feel, to have the space around me filled with another soul. I leaned closer, unable to shatter the pull of his seductive energy.

His gaze dropped to my lips, a moment of

hesitation ripe between us. Then he pulled me to him, capturing my mouth in a kiss. I'd expected it to be brief and forceful, but it wasn't. His lips moved over mine in a gentle caress, asking instead of taking.

So soft, so good, I thought, as I parted my lips beneath his, giving him permission, urging him on.

He needed nothing else. In an instant, everything changed. He opened himself, kissing me with an abandon that I hadn't believed he possessed. My breath caught in my throat as I fell into a desire I'd never experienced. I couldn't think, couldn't reason. I could only feel.

His left hand moved lower, cupping my rear to lift me closer as his right arm tightened around me, cradling me against his chest. His lips moved perfectly with mine, as if we'd kissed countless times. Yet the rush of new discovery pushed me to the edge. His tongue touched mine lightly, like a wand of magic, setting my blood afire. I quivered from the thrill of it, a little moan escaping me. Heat washed over my body, stirring things in me I'd thought long dead. I clutched at his shirt, snaking my arm around his neck. I wanted to-

A door shut upstairs with a discernable creak, then a bang. I jerked away from Adrian, suddenly remembering where we were. I looked at him, startled. His eyes blazed dark and hot, his lips moist from our kisses. I wanted to dive back in, to swim the deep waters until I drowned with bliss. But the creaking door, the door I knew belonged to Lissa's room, brought me up for air. Big time.

I pushed at his shoulder and sat up, then slid to my feet. I stood over him as the ragged sound of our breathing filled the room. There was no sense in denying what had happened. The sharp electricity, the warm heaviness in my body, they said everything. But that was beside the point. I had no business wrapped around this stranger.

No matter how good he looked in moonlight.

He opened his mouth to speak, but I put up a hand in front of him. "You don't have to say you're sorry."

He stood up, his face moving from light into shadow. "Good. I had no intention of apologizing."

I pushed his response away. "It was as much my fault as yours. Let's just forget it and move on."

He took a step closer. The white of his grin gleamed in the darkness. "Are you sure that's what you want?"

No, I wasn't sure. The heat of his body drove me wild, and he wasn't even touching me. I could smell him-a mixture of sweet and spicy, of sweat and sea air. He was all male. I wanted more.

I was losing my mind.

"Yes, that's what I want. My daughters and my sister are upstairs. I think you'd better be on your way. I'll wrap some chicken for you."

With that, I turned and walked to the refrigerator. I pulled out the plate and began tossing chicken legs into a plastic bag, grateful to have my back to him for a few moments so I could catch my breath.

Relief shimmied through me. Yes, this was the right thing. I had too many responsibilities to start tongue wrestling with a man I didn't know the first thing about, except he was tall, gorgeous, and clearly wanted to get inside my clothes as soon as possible.

Oh, yes.

I slammed the door on the Kenmore at the thought and took a big swallow of the nearest drink I could find. Then I started coughing when I realized I'd grabbed a cold glass of Sarabeth's chickory coffee. Black. No sugar. Tree bark in a china cup.

"You okay?" Adrian patted my back as I struggled for air.

I nodded, wishing I could disappear. Was there any possible way I could make a bigger fool of myself?

"Yes, yes. Here's your chicken. Let me walk you to the door," I finally choked out. I couldn't wait to get him out of my hair. I wanted to die of humiliation in peace.

He followed me to the door and waited while I fiddled with the stubborn lock. I almost had him on the front walk when he stopped in the doorframe and turned to me.

"Listen. We got a little ahead of ourselves tonight. Let's start over. Would you like to go out tomorrow night? I want to see you."

I looked up at him, mesmerized by the way the dim light changed his eyes from sky blue to almost cobalt. He seemed so familiar. I couldn't put my finger on it. Why did I feel so natural with him? Why did it feel like coming home when he held me?

This was crazy. With all the chaos going on around us, neither of us had time for insanity. I decided to let him down easy.

"I don't think that's a good idea, Adrian. We're involved together in the investigation. We shouldn't mix personal things with that."

He looked down and moved closer. His dark, musky scent filled my senses again. Delicious.

"You're probably right." His voice, low and soft, caressed my ear. "That would be the smart thing." Then he kissed me, pulling me into his arms as my head went back under the force of his embrace. High voltage shot through me to the tips of my toes. I clung onto his shirt for dear life until he finally let go.

His breathing sounded uneven and harsh in the silence. "But sometimes the smart thing isn't what we ought to do."

"That's true." My fingers still clenched around his collar.

"Six o'clock?"

I took a little gasp of air. "Make it six-thirty."

This time it was me who reached up and pulled him down for a kiss. Then I pushed him away. He was about three seconds from having me jump up, wrap my legs around his waist, and pull him down on the carpet. I shoved him out of the doorway with a muffled "good-bye", then slammed the door.

Damn him if he didn't chuckle on the other side. "Thanks for the chicken."

I leaned back for support and struggled to stay on my feet. My whole body shook, my knees quivered. All from a single kiss. I rubbed my face with my trembling hands. Then stumbled up the stairs to my room for a shower.

I had a date, for the first time in five years. Make that fifteen, if you counted my marriage. All of this at the same time I was trying to save the town from an apparent serial killer.

No one could say my life was boring.

*****

The next morning arrived like the end of a bad dream. I'd tossed and turned all night, unable to sleep with the images of blood in my mind. I felt haunted by the victims, their loss and their suffering. Adrian's kisses and the confusion they stirred only compounded my unease. I finally gave up any pretense of rest and tiptoed down the hall to check on the girls and Izzy.

Since Sean's murder, the girls had chosen to sleep with Izzy in her room, to give her comfort. All three of them were tucked in her huge antique bed, a French Provincial that had once graced our parent's bedroom. My bed had once belonged to my great-great grandparents, Jacob and Marie. Too bad it brought me less luck in love than they experienced.

I left Izzy's door slightly ajar and wandered down the hall, deciding to get a head start on food preparation. Sunday was always a busy day for us, particularly in the summertime when tourists hit the highway.

I glanced at the grandfather clock in the downstairs hallway as I rounded the corner to the family kitchen. Four-fifteen. Janell would be here soon. She'd promised to come by again and help out. But I also knew she'd want an answer about her business plan. I didn't have one. In fact, I hadn't given it a single thought, due to all the turmoil. I hoped she'd understand.

Sarabeth often scolded me about putting up with Janell's occasional self-centeredness. Why did I do it? Because she loved me. When other children told me their mamas wouldn't let them play with a MacPherson, Janell stood by me. When the boys in high school teased me and called me a witch, along with the other word that rhymes with it, Janell threatened to sic her big brother on them. No, she wasn't perfect, but she was fiercely loyal. I valued that in her, above all else. I thought of her business plan and the hard work she'd put into it. Why was I so hesitant to say yes? When had I become that afraid to take a chance?

I pushed open the swinging door, then walked into the restaurant kitchen and clicked on the lights. The pots and pans hung in their places over the huge island prep area. The counters sparkled. Saturday had been a blur of confusion and tumult for me, yet my employees had worked their own magic and made things right. I offered up a prayer of blessing and vowed to repay them.

I'd barely begun to gather the ingredients for that morning's special when I heard Janell drive to the back entrance. The loud blaring of country music announced her arrival. Janell was a Tim McGraw maniac. The stirring chorus to "Live Like You Were Dying" cut off abruptly. Interesting choice of music, considering what was going on in the town over the past two days. I sighed and bent down to pull another set of bowls from under the counter.

"Yoo-hoo," Janell's perky voice sung out. "Anybody up at this hour of the morning?"

"As if I'd ever sleep in. You ready to get to work, indentured servant?"

"You couldn't afford to own me." She tossed her huge straw basket of a purse onto the nearest chair.

"Hey, did you hear about the other murder that happened last night? I was so scared for you. I called, but Sarabeth said you were out."

"Um, yeah. I was out. I was there."

"What? Why didn't Sarabeth tell me? How did you end up in a place like that?"

I laid out the entire story for her, including the meeting with my grandmother and the Cailleach. She sat in the kitchen chair and stared at me until I was done. Then she stood and braced her palms on the white tile of the prep table.

"You have got to be kidding me."

I shook my head as I looked down into the bowl of pancake batter in my hands. "I've never been more serious."

She leaned closer, grabbing my wrist to still the spatula in my hand. "You can't be involved in this, Selene. You're going to get hurt."

A gut reaction deep inside me rose to agree. I ignored it and met her gaze. "I won't get hurt. I have to do this, 'Nell. It's my responsibility. It's part of who I am."

"Forget it. I don't care who died and made you the MacPherson. This is nuts. You said you know the killer saw you. Get out of town. Take Izzy and the kids and run. I mean it." She rubbed her arms as if chilled, the rings on her fingers jangling.

"I can't. I need you to support me, okay?" I tried for a reassuring smile, but I wasn't sure how well I carried it off. "And, I need you to get the bacon ready. We've got customers coming."

Janell opened her mouth to reply, but then shook her head and popped on a pair of rubber gloves. She grabbed the bacon and slapped it into the cast iron skillet, muttering under her breath. I had a feeling today wasn't going to be one of her "pork perfection" days. I'd be lucky if she didn't burn the whole batch.

*****

Before we knew it, it was time to open the doors. I took one last look around the dining room as Bethany and Tammy tied their aprons. They'd beamed under the sunshine of my praise for their work yesterday. My offer of a bonus in their paychecks at the end of the week hadn't hurt matters. I smoothed my hair back, straightened my white lace blouse, and unlocked the door.

Only Mr. Swann stood outside. A handful of the usual regulars hung back in the parking lot, talking to each other as they glanced at the front door. Why weren't they coming in?

It was then that I realized they weren't just slow in approaching. They were watching me, and not in a friendly manner.

Mr. Swann cleared his throat, brushing back his Robert Redford blonde hair with his right hand. "I'm afraid they're a bit concerned after last night. You know, with the latest murder and your, um, presence at the scene."

My hand tightened on the white paint of the door. "I see." My visionary experience had spread through town like wildfire in dry brush. Everything I'd done to erase the old stories had evaporated. I was back to being one of those "weird MacPhersons". Look out, she might belladonna your eggs, or turn you into a toad with a chicory coffee potion.

Tears I'd held inside for so long I didn't think I

remembered how to cry choked at the back of my throat. But I swallowed them down and looked at Mr. Swann. Gratitude swelled in me. He might be my only customer.

His attractiveness edged up several notches as he grinned in return. "I don't know about them, but I'm not going to let anything keep me from the best food in town. Or the prettiest girl."

"Thank you. Come on in and have a seat." My cheeks grew warm beneath his gaze. I knew I was blushing, but it felt so good to have at least one person on my side.

The others watched as I held the door open for Mr. Swann. I tossed them a smile, my head held high, challenging them to think instead of react. It was one of the most difficult "game faces" I'd ever achieved.

The screen door shut behind me as I followed Mr. Swann and Bethany. She seated him at his favorite table, at the back wall next to the window where he sat daily and read newspapers from out of town.

Janell waved at me from the service window. She'd been panting over Mr. Swann for two weeks, pushing me to introduce them. It was definitely time. I smiled at her and jerked my head to come out of the kitchen.

She disappeared from the window in a flash.

With her best "sexy woman" walk in place and her blonde curls bouncing across her high cheekbones, Janell advanced toward us. It was like introducing Marilyn Monroe to Hubble from The Way We Were. All we needed was Barbra Streisand to show up and stage a protest, and we'd have a hit flick on our hands.

"Janell Wilson, I'd like you to meet Mr. Swann." Janell posed for him next to the table. "Mr. Swann, this is Janell Wilson. I'm sorry, I don't know your first name."

"It's Richard." He took Janell's hand and bent over it like an old-time gentleman. "Richard Swann. It's a pleasure to meet you, Miss Wilson. Would you care to join me for breakfast? Apparently the reluctance of our fellow diners means we'll have all the best to ourselves."

"Oh, I have to help out, I'm in the kitchen today, I-" Janell glanced at me with her trademark "deer in the headlights" look.

My only choice was rescue. "Oh, don't be silly. You deserve a lovely breakfast. You've been such a great help. Have a seat. Ya'll enjoy now, y'hear?"

She smiled at me in a way I expect only angels grace their charges, then sat down across from him, reaching over to playfully flick some imaginary lint from his shirt.

His sly smile in response bode well. Lucky Janell.

I nodded and excused myself, knowing this would pay back the countless favors I owed her. A nice feeling, after so much pain.

The bell over the door jingled. I spun around, expectant. I'd hoped to see my regulars traipsing in, one by one. But instead it was a relatively new customer.

Adrian.

My breath caught in my chest. I couldn't deny the part of me that lifted like an eagle at the sight of him. I knew it was dangerous to have these feelings. I knew how horrific the crash to earth would be. But he was here, when others stayed away.

I walked toward him. His little half-grin brightened his face when he saw me.

"Hey."

Amazing what the man could do with just a word. I wanted so badly to throw my arms around him, to feel the wholeness I felt when he touched me. But I held back, keeping a proper distance.

"Hey, yourself. Taking a chance, coming to the witch's gingerbread house, aren't you? You might find yourself in my oven." I glanced out the window at my customers, still clustered in a group at the far end of the pavement. What were they waiting for? Another dead body to drop from sky at my feet? Maybe they'd prefer Dorothy to drop a Kansas farmhouse on me instead.

Adrian followed my gaze and sighed. "I see the rumor mill is up and running. I'm sorry, Selene. I didn't fully realize how much your helping us would affect things. No one would have batted an eye in Chicago. Well, beyond the usual ribbing and joking."

"It's a different world down here." Talk about an understatement. I reached up and ran a hand down his shirtsleeve to soothe him. It wasn't his fault. I'd chosen to expose myself. "You won't have it any better, Adrian. The mayor and the town council will question your judgment. I should have thought of that before I agreed, but I was too busy —"

"Doing the right thing."

His look was so protective and fierce I had to smile. "Well, come on. I bet you're hungry. We've got plenty. Buffet-style today?"

"You bet." He slipped an arm around my waist,

and for once, I didn't fight it as he gave me a brief hug.

I glanced over his shoulder to see Janell and Mr. Swann rise from the table. He threw down far too much money in payment on the table, and then took Janell's hand as they walked toward the door. She waggled her fingers at me and mouthed the words "bless you" as she followed him.

I led Adrian to a table, then walked to the window and watched as Janell and Mr. Swann—I supposed I should call him Richard now—climbed into his dark blue Honda. I knew I should be happy, ecstatic that my best friend had what she wanted. But I couldn't. A dull, distant unease moved in like a sea fog over my spirit and refused to lift.

I tried to shake off the disquiet. *There you go again, Selene. Another overreaction.* I'd seen more than I'd ever bargained for during the past few days. It was sure to have an effect on me. It was probably just delayed stress.

I let the white lace curtain fall back into place and told myself to focus on the day ahead. But I couldn't shake the discomfort. Nothing felt right.

I wasn't sure it ever would again.

Chapter Eight

Help came from an unexpected source.

"Get your bony carcass in there, Lamont Sweeney. If you think I'm gonna feed you and your cronies breakfast, you've got another think comin'.."

I spun from the window to spy Odette Sweeney as she shooed her husband and his friends in the front door. They shot me a sidelong glance but obeyed as they trudged to their usual table beneath the chandelier.

Odette approached me, the scent of Hawaiian White Ginger following her like a sweet companion. She enveloped me in a bosomy hug and patted my back.

"How you doin', my girl?" She held me away from her, her sharp gaze missing nothing. She shook her head in commiseration. "Just like your Granny, you are." She clucked her tongue at me. "You just don't know it yet."

"It's good to see you." I finally allowed myself to smile. Odette had been my Grandmother's closest friend and only true champion. She rarely left her house anymore, content to stay home and knit blankets for her great-grandchildren. I didn't have to ask what drew her out of her retreat today.

"Well, I couldn't sit around and let the busybodies have at you, could I? Particularly when one of them is my own Lamont. I swear, he and his buddies are worse than a henhouse full of chickens."

I threw my arms around Odette and blessed the

heavens. She hugged me back and pulled away as she swept into action.

"Lamont, what are you waiting for? Get me a plate of food, sugar. You, Arnold James, where's your wife? Get her on that new-fangled cell phone of yours and have her bring our coffee group over here. We're havin' a feast today."

Odette chuckled as she watched Lamont rush to the buffet table, plate in hand. "Trained him good, I did. But I love him to dickens." She winked at me, then walked toward the table of men, a sovereign among her subjects.

One by one, the restaurant began to fill. By ten it was at usual capacity. Highway travelers mingled with locals, crisp Boston accents mixed with Texas twang, California girls met Georgia peaches.

I stood by the kitchen door and smiled. What a difference a little hurricane named Odette could bring. But for the townspeople and the handful of vacationers who'd remained in Fort Bedford after the Festival cancellation, the conversations were low, serious, and of a definitely murderous quality.

"First Sean Nelson. Now that tourist boy from Mobile, he was the second one. It's shameful. So who do you think did it?" Lamont took another bite of grits from his third plate of food and looked up at me.

Bottomless pits like Lamont made me question the profitability of going buffet-style. "I don't know." I cleared a few of the plates scattered around the pulled-together tables.

"How come? Ain't you a voodoo queen, like your Grandma?"

There was more than a hint of accusation in

Arnold James's question, but I chose to ignore it. "My grandmother didn't practice voodoo and you know it." I shook my head at him as if he were a child in need of correction. "No, I don't know who did it, but I think we'd all be better off taking extra care and precautions for the time being."

Many of the older people in Fort Bedford still left their doors and windows unlocked. I wondered what Adrian would think at that bit of news. We were a far cry from the streets of Chicago.

"Humph." Arnold shrugged his shoulders, but I knew his downcast gaze meant he'd heard my suggestion.

"Selene's right." Odette pointed at me with her fork. "We need to band together and face this thing head on, watch out for each other. I think we should organize a neighborhood watch."

"Good idea. I know just the man to help you on that." I glanced at Adrian as he finished his breakfast. He'd told me he was in a hurry to get back to the station, but I knew this was an opportunity to obtain the support of one of the most influential women in the town. An ally he might need when he faced the town council.

"Be right back." I turned from the table and walked to Adrian's side.

He gave me a slow, easy grin. "Ready for tonight?"

I glanced at the crowd watching us, then shook my head. "I don't think it's a good idea. We've attracted enough attention already. I don't think it would do either of us any good to be seen about town."

He leaned forward and lowered his voice. "Don't worry. I have something private planned. No one will see us."

I drew a finger across the edge of his table, unable to stop the pleasure his words stirred. I loved it when he spoke like that, like a midnight phone call on a sultry night. It felt like warm honey, slipping south over my skin.

"Private, huh?   Should I bring Sarabeth to chaperone?"

He wiped his mouth on the linen napkin and chuckled. "I like her a lot, and she's a hell of a cook. Not as good as you, of course. No, you're safe with me. At least...as safe as you want to be." He looked up, his eyes lit with mischief. And something more.

It was that something more I couldn't refuse, even if I should. "Okay. Six-thirty. Oh, by the way, I need you to come and meet Odette Sweeney. Trust me, you'll be glad you did."

"Really? Why?"

"Every brave knight needs a patroness."

*****

"I can't believe you're going out on a date with a killer on the loose."

"Well, I can't either." I twisted to the side as I tied the sash of my dress. "I know this is ridiculous, but look at it this way. How could I be any safer than with the Chief of Police? It's like having a bodyguard for the evening."

"Not likely." Sarabeth walked behind me, inspecting my choice of clothes for the evening. I'd gone for a simple black wrap dress and my strappy black sandals. I had no idea what the dress code was to this "somewhere private," and Adrian wouldn't tell me. This would have to do. I left my long, dark hair loose and wavy. It had gone too wild to fight it tonight.

"You shouldn't be going at all. Sean's funeral is Tuesday. You ought to be here with Izzy."

I turned to Sarabeth and nodded. "I know, but she already told me that she was going to spend time with Sean's family this evening. She won't be home until late."

Sarabeth crossed her arms over her chest and scowled.

I mirrored her stance. "Why don't you tell me what's really the matter? Get it all out on the table. What's changed? I thought you liked him."

"I do. He's a good man. I could see that when he was here. But I saw other things, too. He isn't telling you the full truth about himself, Selene. Be cautious. He's more than he appears."

"Aren't we all." I turned toward the mirror and picked up a gold hoop earring.

"Yes, but he's got secrets, *ma petite.*"

I looked at her reflection in the mirror as she stood behind me. "Oh? Are you going to tell me what they are?"

"I'm not that good, *bebe.* Sensing things like that is your department."

I grinned and finished putting on the second earring. "That's debatable. Don't worry about me, all right? I thought you wanted me to date. What about all those men you've trotted through the house the past five years?"

"That was different! I've known most of those boys since they were in diapers, and so have you."

I turned and patted her cheek. "Did it ever occur to you that fact might have been the very thing that turned me off?"

Sarabeth's brows gathered over her dark, sherry-colored eyes. "Oh."

"Precisely. Adrian's different, Sarabeth. He's a new adventure, and I've-well, I've never had one of those. Let me enjoy it for a little while, okay?"

She blew out a frustrated breath, but finally nodded. "All right. I'll be with the girls, so call me if you need me to come...you know, pick you up."

I laughed. "You mean if he dumps me alongside the road or I leave him at the dinner table? I'll get home in one piece, I promise."

Sarabeth grabbed my hand and held it tight. "The Three of Swords is still the present energy, my girl. Don't you forget it. Not even for a sweet-talkin' man."

I sobered and hugged her. "I'll be careful. Please don't worry. The Cailleach is with me."

Sarabeth hugged me one last time, then released me. "I hope that's enough."

I kissed her cheek, then grabbed my black woven shawl and slipped it over my shoulders. Even in June, Fort Bedford could be cool in the evening, when the ocean breeze swept across darkened dunes and through the streets.

Steph and Lissa walked in at that moment, forgetting to knock as usual. I'd been surprised in my underwear more than once and admonished them to change their habit of barging in unannounced, but it never seemed to take.

"Wow, sexy legs, Mom. Where are you going like that?"

I gave Steph's long blonde hair a playful pull. "Don't be talking like that to your Mama. I'm just going out with a friend."

"Mr. Burke," Lissa piped up, her gaze curious and inspecting. I wondered for a moment what she saw in my aura, and if she understood it. Anxiety? Fear? Overworked hormones? I groaned within, wishing for the millionth time that none of us had been born into a magical family.

"That guy? You're going out on a date, Mom?" Steph's expression reflected her aversion to the idea. I knew it would have been smarter to tell the girls about the date, but Sarabeth persuaded me to keep it private. Steph still harbored the fantasy that Jason would come back one day and sweep us off to his fairy kingdom. I knew that was never going to happen. Sarabeth felt it wasn't fair to rub her nose in the truth. Yet how much fairer was it to lie?

"He's just a friend, Stephie."

She looked down, her customary sullen expression restored. I'd made the wrong choice with her. Again.

I turned to Lissa and forced a smile as I bent down. "And how did you know he was the friend I meant, Miss Priss?"

"That's easy. I saw his colors and yours. They match. The same kind of red and pink. Really pretty."

I stood up, the smile frozen on my face. Passion and love colors. Sarabeth lifted her eyebrows at me, her face a vision of "I told you so." I shook my head at her.

Similar colors between us? That didn't mean I had to give in to them. "I'll only be gone a little while. Lock all the doors and windows and don't play outside tonight, okay? Stay inside with Sarabeth."

The girls nodded. Lissa threw her arms around me and I bent to kiss her, lifting my spirits. Steph offered me her cheek, then turned and walked down the hall to her room, slamming the door. I sighed and vowed to have a long and much-needed conversation with her tomorrow.

I walked to the staircase and took the first step as the doorbell rang. I glanced behind me and saw Sarabeth and Lissa peeking through my bedroom door. I shooed at them with my hand and grinned. Lissa giggled as the door shut.

The hem of my shirt swished around my knees when I walked down the stairs. I practically lived in jeans and long broomstick skirts. This sleek outfit had been worn one other time before I shoved it to the back of my closet with the rest of my old dreams. Maybe it was time to dust a few of those off and see what happened.

I opened the front door, a lump of nervousness fixed in my belly. It didn't get any easier when I saw what awaited me. Adrian stood, dressed in his black leather jacket and jeans, a red button-down shirt beneath. His hair, windblown and casual, curled just a bit below his ears. In his hands was a small bouquet of pink gladiolas. My favorite. "How did you know?" I took the flowers from him.

He smiled and motioned behind him. "You have them all over the front walk here. Besides, they remind me of you."

"Oh? How so?" I lifted the bouquet to my face, brushing the soft petals against my skin.

"They're strong and beautiful. But soft and full of grace."

"You're good at this." Oh yes. He was very, very good.

"You think so? I've been practicing that line for an hour." Then he laughed, the expression in his eyes merry.

That was it. Throw caution to the winds, I decided. At least for one night.

*****

When Adrian said private, he meant it. We climbed into his truck and barreled down the highway heading east, away from the familiarity of Fort Bedford. I asked him several times where we were going, but he only laughed and said it was a surprise.

A bit of apprehension drifted through my mind. I was traveling away from home with a man I knew very little about, and one whom Sarabeth confirmed held secrets in his heart. But didn't we all have secrets? I shook off the vestiges of dread and tried to recall what it had been like the last time I was carefree. It took me a while to remember. Not a good sign.

"Penny for your thoughts." He sounded like Humphrey Bogart in Casablanca. Why did all my personal references come from classic old movies? Maybe I harbored a few strange secrets, too.

"I was trying to recall the last time I let my hair down and did something crazy. Let's just say it's been a long time."

He chuckled. "Oh, yeah? Tell me about it. I think the last time for me was tenth grade."

I laughed. The wind from his rolled-down truck window whipped my mane into a wild dance and I dragged a lock of hair from my eyes. I'd end up looking like a she-devil by the time we arrived at...wherever it was. "Tenth grade, huh? That does it. You have to go first."

He grinned, his hands strong and sure on the wheel. Something about the way he drove was so damned sexy. Just looking at him sent my blood pressure shooting skyward.

"Okay. It was the night of the junior-senior prom. My sister got dumped by her boyfriend at the last minute for some cheerleader. So I set off with my friends on a vendetta."

"Ooooh, vendetta. How very Michael Corleone of you."

"My friends thought so. We hung out and waited until my sister's boyfriend and his date showed up and went inside. Then we-well, I'm ashamed to say it now."

"What? What did you do?"

"We broke into his car and smeared the seats with dog poop. The seats were dark leather, so you couldn't see the special coating. But you could sure smell it."

I laughed, slapping Adrian on the arm. "You evil, evil boy. I'll bet you stuck around to see the show, didn't you?"

He grinned again and dragged a hand through his hair. "Yeah, we did. It was hilarious. They unlocked the door and almost fell over from the stench. Then he got inside the car, looking for the source, and...well, let's just say he discovered the source spread all over his rented tuxedo. It was the talk of Roselle, Illinois for years."

I grinned, amazed by this side of him. "Did your sister enjoy the news?"

"You bet. But we never told anyone it was us. Not even her. In fact, I've never told anyone the truth about that story-except you." He smiled and gazed out the windshield, a bit of reserve returning to his energy. I realized his embarrassment at revealing a skeleton in his closet. I sensed he held other specters at bay and didn't like this break of custom. An urge to equal the scales settled over me.

I reached across the bench seat of the truck and laid a hand on his arm. "Are you ready to hear mine?"

"You bet." Some of his earlier ease returned to his expression.

"Well, since you revealed a deep, dark, teenaged secret, I guess I'll have to tell you one of mine. It's about the first—and last—time I cast a love spell."

"Love spell, huh? Are you really a witch like they say?"

I shook my head. "I don't like that word. It brings to mind wicked, green-warty hags who eat children and curse the crops. My people were what my Irish ancestors called the Aes Dana...the people of Dana. The people of inspiration. Poets, bards, druids, magicians, wise women. We worked for the good of others, not their downfall. Not unless they deserved the payback, that is."

He looked at me, a sly grin on his face. "I have no idea what you're talking about, but I like the concept. So, who was this love spell directed toward? Some seventh-grade dream guy?"

"Hardly. Actually, you know who it was. It was Jake."

"Jake Carlisle? You're kidding. Why would you want him? I mean, not to put him down, but Jake?"

I laughed and watched Adrian try to wiggle out from under his social gaffe. "Hey, in ninth grade, Jake was hot stuff. He didn't become insufferable until later."

Adrian grinned and nodded. "Go on."

I sat back in my seat and glanced out the windshield. The shore was to my right, but it didn't look familiar. Where were we? "I decided Jake was the man for me. So I gathered the proper herbs and stones, and under a full moon I chanted for him to fall in love with me. Even though he saw me as the worst kind of annoying brat. I was two years younger than he."

"Poor Selene. Unrequited love."

"Yes, a sad, sad story. So anyway, I cast the spell. And it worked, too. Except I learned why Granny always told me not to cast a love spell on a particular person, especially one who doesn't like you in the first place."

Adrian glanced at me with curiosity. "Why?"

"Because what you end up with is a guy who's in love with you and doesn't want to be. And that leads to only one thing."

"Great sex?"

I laughed and shoved his shoulder. "No! You end up with a very irritated suitor. Jake finally called me and said, 'You want to go out with me or what, MacPherson? I don't wanna go, but I can't stop myself from asking.' True romance, let me tell you."

"So what did you finally do?"

I leaned back in my seat and smiled. "I went to Granny, and after a lengthy lecture and a month-long list of chores to do in repayment, we reversed the spell and set Jake free. He's always teased me about love spells, though. Something inside told him the truth, even though he doesn't believe it. I learned my lesson. I've never used magic since."

Adrian turned right and drove down a darkened side road. "Are you sure that's the lesson your grandmother wanted you to take from it? To never work magic again?"

"I don't know. I only know that's the one I received. Anyway, no one but Granny ever knew about this, until now. We're even."

Adrian parked at the end of the pavement and shut off the engine. The car interior dropped into darkness.

He turned toward me and rested his forearm on the seat behind my head. "I guess we'll just have to trust each other with this information, won't we."

I leaned back and looked at him. "I guess so."

The moment lingered between us, as fine and tenuous as a spider's web. Finally a smile spread across both our faces. He pulled away and unlocked his door.

"Ready for dinner?"

I glanced around me. "Where?"

"Right here." He exited the truck and motioned toward the sea. "Welcome to the House of Adrian. Observe."

He reached behind his crew-cab seat and pulled out a large duffle bag. Then he came to my side of the truck and opened my door.

"Right this way, madam. We have reservations."

"Oh, really? Who did you make them with? Poseidon?"

He took my hand and led me to the beach. "Unbeliever."

Fortunately for us, the wind had calmed a bit with the sunset. He pulled a blanket from the bag and spread it on the sand. A couple of pillows and a lantern with matches followed.

"Boy, you came equipped." I tried to keep my tone light. Knowing how much thought he'd put into this outing on short notice was far too powerful an aphrodisiac for me.

He lit the lantern. A soft glow encircled us.

"We haven't gotten to the best part." He reached further into the bag and pulled out the last thing I expected. A large, square-shaped insulated bag. A pizza warmer.

He opened the bag with a flourish, then pulled out a box from Florian's Pizzeria. "Double pepperoni. With beer, ice cold."

"A man after my own heart."

He whipped out a tiny ice chest and cracked open a beer for me. I dug into a thick, cheesy slice of heaven.

We ate and laughed and counted the stars

overhead, until the entire pizza was gone and my beer disappeared. Adrian drank a soda instead, since he was driving. I volunteered to drink his beer for him. He let me.

While Adrian left to dispose of the trash, I lay back on the blanket, the warmth of the alcohol loosening my muscles as well as a few of my inhibitions. The wind threw my skirt up over my thighs, but I didn't care. It felt glorious, like being a part of the wind and the sea itself. I reached over my head and stretched like a cat. The softness of the blanket and the giving caress of the sand beneath me acted like a cloud of pleasure to my senses. I'd never felt so free, so good.

Adrian returned, and then stood looking down at me. At last he dropped to his knees beside me. He waited, unmoving, as if he refused to budge without my invitation. The wind blew his hair, giving him the look of a lover and a warrior at the same time.

Again I had the sense of familiarity, a kind of knowing that didn't make sense. I reached out, caressing his thigh with my hand. Somehow I knew where to touch him, what would please him. I reached up and boldly grabbed his belt buckle, then pulled him to lie with me.

He moved to my side and drew me into his arms, burrowing his face in the wild mass of my hair. His lips traveled down the curve of my neck as his hand swept over my body. The tie to my dress came undone, but I didn't care. His hand moved the thin dress aside and he cupped my lace-covered breast in his hand.

I pushed up against him, wanting all he could

give. I knew I should be more cautious, more careful. This was foolish. But I didn't care. I hadn't felt a man's desire in so long. I hadn't realized how much I had missed it until now. A hot, shimmering delight flooded through me as I let go and gave myself to him.

"Selene." His kisses trailed down the upper curve of my breast and his hand eased the thin material of my bra out of his way. The cool wind swept over my skin, tightening the pink bud to hardness. It was almost painful, but then the hot, wet warmth of his tongue swept over it, removing all thoughts of anything but him. I cried out, digging my hands into his hair. At first I thought to push him away. But instead I held his head closer, urging him on as his hand moved lower, skimming over the smooth skin of my belly.

"Adrian." My voice sounded rough and hoarse to my ears.

"Yes...say my name, Selene." His tongue returned to dance around the tight, dark circle of pleasure at my breast.

"Adrian," I sighed, nearer to his ear. He growled with a sound of desire, then pulled the wet bud deep into his mouth, sucking harder. I almost leapt from the sand in response. Had I ever experienced anything as remotely powerful as this? If I had, it couldn't possibly compare to this sensual plunder. I was being taken. And I wanted it to happen.

Adrian's hand slipped beneath the elastic band of my panties, edging his way closer and closer to the one place I wanted him most. I rocked my hips against his hand, showing him how badly I wanted him, how much I needed him. He moved his body over mine. The feel of his long, hard weight on my body was the most delicious pressure, the sweetest burden.

"Yes, yes." My head spun in a universe not my own. I opened my legs and moved to let him-

The loud blare of his police radio broke us apart with a jerk. We gazed over our heads at the truck as if it was an alien craft. The radio signal sounded again, followed by some unintelligible chatter that didn't make sense.

"Damn." Adrian rolled from me. He gazed at me for a long moment as the cool wind swept over my partially nude body. I knew I should be ashamed, that I should cover myself, but I wanted him to look. It felt right to give him that. It felt right to give him everything, and I didn't know why.

"God, you're so beautiful, Selene. I never imagined it could be like..."

The radio sounded again, like an insistent child who would not be denied.

"I have to get that." Regret weighed heavy in his voice.

"I know." A part of me mourned the loss of what we'd begun.

He rose with some difficulty and walked toward the truck.

I sat up, pulling my bra back into place with a shaking hand. I could still feel his lips there, tugging at the nipple and bringing me closer to orgasm than I'd been in years. I shivered, but not from the cold. I tied the sash at the side of my waist and pulled myself back together as well as I could when he returned, his face ashen and serious.

A sense of dread coursed down my spine at the sight of him. "What is it?"

He put his hands on his thighs as he knelt next to me. "They've found another body, Selene. We have to get back."

"Oh, God, no. Not another one. Who-where?"

"The body hasn't been positively identified. They found him at Raven's Beach. Not far from your house."

Raven's Beach.

The same beach where I'd seen the Cailleach.

Chapter Nine

I wrapped my shawl tight around my shoulders as we arrived at the crime scene, already bright with lights for the investigation. Johnny, the young officer who'd interviewed Izzy at the bar, headed our way across the sand as soon as he spied Adrian's truck.

"Chief, we-oh, hey, Ms. MacPherson." Johnny's eyes filled with surprise when he caught sight of me. "Chief, we need you to get down there as soon as possible. We haven't touched the body yet. It's the same as the other two. Face down in the sand, knife wounds in the back. Six fingers missing, this time. Some kind of weird message in that."

Adrian opened his glove compartment and pulled out a pair of latex gloves. "Leaving a message isn't uncommon for serial killers."

His gaze fixed on the shoreline where his men gathered. The light from the compartment glinted off the smooth, tight burn scars on his hand as he pulled on the gloves. It hit me that I hadn't seen him in anything but long-sleeved shirts, even though it was summertime.

He turned to me. "Stay here. Don't leave the truck." His expression was remote and serious, a far cry from the laughing man who'd counted the stars and brought me pizza, beer, and passion only a half hour ago.

A part of me drew back from him, disconcerted. "All right."

He paused for a moment, as if considering his actions. Then he leaned over and kissed me, a brief, hard kiss that told me that somewhere underneath the Chief, the other man still existed.

Johnny gazed at me with his eyebrows lifted as Adrian exited the truck. Guess Johnny hadn't seen that one coming. So much for keeping the nature of our relationship a secret. I knew Adrian had done it to assuage my fears. He was right. I was afraid, on many levels, and not just because a killer stalked Fort Bedford.

He walked across the sand, talking with Johnny as more patrol cars appeared. Even though Adrian had been off duty tonight, would he be criticized for traveling a half hour away at a time like this? In the company of the controversial Selene MacPherson? This wasn't going to be good, for either of us.

I pushed the thoughts of what the town might say out of my mind. What was I doing? Someone lay dead on the beach. That was the only thing that mattered right now. I could see the victim's back, a rumpled blue jean jacket covered with blood.

A shiver shook me as a cool, familiar presence entered my aura. I hadn't felt a sensation like that since the night my mother came to visit me, three days after her death.

A soul was in attendance.

I closed my eyes and calmed, envisioning strong, silver roots encircling my feet. I mentally sent the roots deep into the sand, then further into the ground below me. I needed strong anchoring to the Earth. Then I opened myself to listen.

"I'm here. What can I do to help you?"

Granny taught me as a child that many souls don't communicate well. They send you what they

can. Images, smells, parts of sentences. This one was
no different. I saw flashes of light, dizzying images of
the sea. I could smell a man's aftershave lotion, a
scent that seemed recognizable. The words "can't get
away" and "help me" floated in my mind. My heart
went out for the soul, most likely the murder victim,
still present in the area and not sure what to do. At
least on that level, I could help. I knew how to-

In that instant, a knife penetrated me, over and
over. I cried out as hot, searing pain flooded my
senses, cutting my breath. The feeling of blood
flowing over my clothes and down my back in a
torrent shook me from my trance. My eyes flew open,
and I half-expected to see the murderer in the truck
with me.

No one was there. I checked my body for
wounds, even though I knew it couldn't be real. My
eyes filled with tears as the intense pain in my back
began to fade and my mind cleared.

This was different. Before, I'd felt the impact of
the force used to drive the knife into the body. This
time I'd been given the full experience. The impact,
the pain, the blood loss. This soul had chosen to share
with me its final moment. And then I knew why.

I opened the truck door and got out, my sandals
sinking into the sand. I slipped them off and threw
them into the cab, then slammed the door. It took a
bit of doing to trudge across loose sand. The night air
cooled it, making that part of the trek a little easier. I
slid down the side of a small sand dune, as I'd seen
Adrian do earlier. Then I approached the crime scene.

Johnny rushed forward. "Hey, you can't come
down here."

"Try and stop me," I choked out, faking to the left and then circling around him to the right.

"Hey." He grabbed my arm just as Harlan turned to me, tears in his eyes.

"Selene." Johnny let me go and I embraced Harlan.

Jake was dead.

Jake Carlisle, his best friend and partner. My first girlhood crush.

"I'm so sorry."

I wasn't sure he heard me over the sound of the waves. Harlan had been one of the few boys in high school to refuse to join in with the teasing and name-calling toward me. He and Jason and Jake. The town called them The Three Musketeers. Jake used to laugh and call them The Three Muscatels instead, after the cheap wine he'd stolen from his Daddy's liquor cabinet.

So innocent. So long ago.

The headlights from other cars flashed above us. The inner urge to hide and do it quickly blinked in my mind. I let go of Harlan and ran behind a sand dune, just as the new arrivals exited their vehicles.

The mayor and a few of the town councilmen stumbled their way down the sand dunes. From the looks of them, it had been a long time since they'd been forced to engage in this much physical activity. Soft and fleshy, their only exercise consisted in controlling whatever they could in Fort Bedford County.

"Chief Burke!" Mayor O'Neill ordered.

Adrian crouched over Jake's body, directing his men. He didn't lift his head when the Mayor bellowed. Either the wind had snatched the sound away or he was ignoring the old blowhard.

"Chief Burke." the mayor yelled again, louder this time. Adrian stood and faced him.

I held still, afraid to be discovered. I knew the mayor could turn my presence into a weapon to use against Adrian.

"This investigation is out of your hands, Burke. This is Lieutenant Andrews of the Florida State Police. You'll take your orders from him, as of now."

Adrian nodded to the stern, older man in the dark blue suit. They exchanged words, but I couldn't hear them over the roar of the sea. The older man motioned with his hands. A group of his officers descended, scattering like birds fighting over bread crumbs at the park.

One of the men tossed Harlan some stakes and a roll of yellow crime scene tape and motioned to him to get to work. Harlan stood a moment, staring down at the tape in his hands. Then he glanced at me, his eyes dark with memory of Jake and his infamous rope barricades.

I gave him a small smile. I remembered, too.

Harlan turned away and set himself to the task. I eyed the investigators closely. Once I saw they were fully occupied, I doubled back over the dunes and returned to the truck.

I opened the truck door and climbed in, wiping the sand from my legs and feet and slipping my shoes back on. Maybe Adrian wouldn't know what I'd done.

"Get a good view of the crime scene?"

I shrieked in surprise, then saw Adrian in the

darkness next to the opened door. How had he trailed me without my knowledge? "Don't scare me like that." I pulled my legs into the truck and faced forward.

Adrian stepped closer and rolled down the window, then slammed the door shut. "I told you to stay in the truck. Why did you disobey me?" He clenched his fists, anger shimmering around him in waves.

I pulled back, disturbed by the intensity of his emotion. "I had to. I knew it was Jake."

He started to speak, but then stopped. He didn't have to ask how I knew. A long, steady sigh slipped from his lips. Then he slammed his hands on the car door, frustration rolling from him. "Dammit! We're no closer to the identity of the killer than we were on Friday. He's up to one murder a day and we don't have anything material on him. The town is going to dissolve into a panic when this news hits the fan."

His next words hung in the air unspoken, but it wasn't too hard to pick up on their energy. I could almost hear his self-accusation ring in his mind. *It's my fault.* I reached up through the window and ran my fingers into his hair. He closed his eyes and turned his face into my palm for a moment, rubbing his cheek against the curve of my hand.

"I have to get back." He pushed away from the door. "Here's the keys. Take the truck to your house. I'll come by and get it later." He turned away, a shroud of icy withdrawal cloaking him.

"Adrian."

He looked back, the wind tossing his dark hair over his forehead.

I took the risk. "I'll be waiting for you."

*****

It was almost midnight by the time a patrol car dropped Adrian at my home. I sat on the front porch, the light of the still-full moon overhead. He spoke briefly to the officer in the vehicle and watched as it drove away.

The tall, dark silhouette of his body as he walked slowly toward the house increased the sorrow already filling my heart. Defeat and failure walked with him like ghostly sentinels. He strode past me in the shadows, approaching the front door.

"Adrian. Here I am."

He turned toward me. "I didn't see you there."

"I know. Come sit with me." I patted the empty seat on the porch swing.

He hesitated, then finally came closer and dropped his weary frame on the cushion.

I passed him a cold glass of water. He drank it down in a few gulps, then leaned back. "That was just what I needed. But you knew that, didn't you?" He grinned slightly.

"No. I'm not that good, as Sarabeth likes to say. But a cold drink would be the first thing I'd want after a night like this."

Adrian laid his head on the back of the swing and looked up at the porch ceiling. I reached over and took his hand.

What could I do? His pain was so great. Without thinking, I said the first thing that came to my mind. "Tell me another secret. I'll tell you mine."

He snorted, his gaze still on the ceiling. "Which

one? I've got so many."

I stopped trying to figure him out and opened myself to his energy. "Tell me the hardest one to hold inside."

"No contest. That would be the night Madelyn died."

"Your girlfriend?"

"No. My wife."

His answer stopped me cold. "I didn't know you'd been married."

"Yeah. She was my college girlfriend. So beautiful, inside and out. One of those long, cool blondes. I used to tease her and call her Gwyneth, after Gwyneth Paltrow." He grinned, his eyes hazy with memory.

I tried to avoid comparing my small, dark looks to his memories of a blonde princess. I almost succeeded.

"We'd been married about three years when it happened. It was Christmas Eve. We were driving to her parent's house in Palatine. So damn cold that night. Wet, too. I let her open her present from me early. I told her she'd need it that night."

I nodded. "Yes, the coat." The image of the grey, fox fur-trimmed jacket filled my mind. The vision I'd seen was so crisp, so real. Madelyn laughing, enjoying his company, basking in the light of his love.

Until she died.

Adrian's energy shifted, slipping into a gloomy darkness. I held tighter to his hand and followed him there.

"I didn't see it. I should have. I'm a cop. I'm supposed to be on watch, all the time. But I only saw her. She was teasing me, laughing about how extravagant I'd been. She said buying her a real fur guaranteed me a present I'd never forget, as soon as we got home."

He swallowed hard. "It was black ice. The kind that forms on the roadway, but you can't see it. I could have avoided it. I didn't."

I braced myself for what I knew would come.

"We slid. I used every skill I'd learned in the academy to pull us free. I could have done it, too. Except for the other car that crossed the intersection behind us and took the same slide. We swung around and hit, head-on."

He pulled his hand from mine and sat forward on the swing, his elbows on his knees. "The other car. It was a woman and a little girl. They weren't wearing their seatbelts. They were thrown on impact when the car overturned. Killed."

He hung his head low. "Madelyn, she had her seatbelt on. So did I. But she hit the side window, hard. So much blood. I was hurt, too, but somehow I managed to stay conscious. I tried to get her out of the car, but it was too mangled around her legs. Then the fire started."

A single sob broke free from his chest. I leaned forward and embraced him, but he didn't seem to know I was there.

"The people at the scene pulled me out. I fought them off, even after my clothes caught fire. I kept screaming for Madelyn. They wouldn't let me go. I could see the other victims sprawled in the street. I couldn't do anything. Madelyn. She never woke up. They never got her out. I-oh God, they stood by and they let her burn. They wouldn't let me go."

The sobs shook him as he finally released his demons. I held him tight, mingling my own tears with his. Seeing the vision of what had happened was nothing compared to the blinding agony inside his heart and mind.

He pushed me away and stood, dragging a shaky hand through his hair. "It's happening again. People are dead and I can't stop it."

I rose beside him and grabbed his arm. "Are you blaming yourself for these killings? You can't."

He shook off my hand, jerking his arm free. "Stay away from me, Selene. For your own good. I mean it."

With that, he snatched his car keys from the white wicker table next to us and strode across the porch. The truck roared to life and he sped away, kicking up a cloud of dust that reminded me of smoke as it lifted from the driveway.

I stood on the porch for a long time, watching the cloud return to the Earth in a gentle wave. Adrian had recovered from his physical injuries, but the energy he drew behind him wasn't death.

It was pain.

*****

Everything was different the next day. Even Odette lacked the power to control the storm descending upon us.

The restaurant was full that Monday morning. Not because the food was especially good. I'd lacked the energy to put out anything but the most pedestrian fare. No, the restaurant was full because the locals had decided to turn it into the headquarters of Hysteria Central. I couldn't blame them.

Leanna Mitchell hugged her baby close to her chest. "I think the governor should call out the National Guard."

"Forget the National Guard. I want the Army in here. Homeland Security, whatever it takes." Lamont shifted his gaze across the faces of the people gathered around him.

"At least the State is in charge now, not that worthless Chief Burke." Marjorie Simmons shoved a forkful of sausage into her mouth for emphasis.

"Yeah. Who the hell brought that Yankee down here in the first place?" Arnold James banged on the table with his fist. "First thing, I want the mayor to fire his ass."

The others agreed, murmuring support.

I stood by the buffet table, trapped like an animal in a cage.

If I stood up for Adrian, it could go badly for him. The endorsement of the "town witch" wasn't exactly a plus to some of these people. I wasn't sure if the rumors about the kiss Johnny witnessed had made the rounds yet. If they had, then the best thing I could do was keep low and stay quiet. Yet if I didn't speak up for someone I cared for, what kind of woman was I?

I glanced at my feet, crossing my arms. I did care for Adrian. I could at least admit that. I wasn't sure how much. Not yet.

I lifted my head and grabbed the platter of hash browns next to me. "Here's the last of them for the day, gang. Eat up." I placed the tray in the middle of the gathered tables.

"What do you think about all this, Selene?" Odette looked up at me, her gleaming white hair piled high in an old-fashioned beehive.

I took a quick breath. Then I dove in. "I think we shouldn't jump to conclusions about anything or anyone. We don't have all the information. But I do think we should gather together and keep one another safe. That's the old way. I think it's still the right one."

I could feel their gazes like physical touches on my skin, their energies coming at me from all directions. It was unnerving. "I also think we need to take care of the Nelsons, the Carlisles, and everyone around us who's in mourning today."

"Amen," Missy Watson's dark brown curls swept forward as she bowed her head. Missy was Odette's daughter, born only a few months before my mother.

"That's my Selene. Always the voice of reason." Odette took another bite of her biscuit as the table quieted.

"That ain't what I heard." Arnold James leaned back in his chair like a stuffed canary.

I lifted my gaze to him. Muddy red colors washed his aura so intensely, even I could see it. Negative energy spiked the air around him like small daggers. He had a bee in his bonnet this time. The stinger was meant for me.

"I heard her and the chief been gettin' pretty cozy. I wouldn't take her word for much about him." He flashed a smug grin at his enrapt audience.

All eyes fixed on me.

"He's become a friend of the family." I knew how weak I sounded.

"A friend of the MacPhersons. Well, if that don't say it all, I don't know what does," Arnold crossed his thick, beefy arms. A few of the others snickered.

Odette scowled at him. "Watch your p's and q's, Arnold   James."

Arnold shrugged, a triumphant expression on his face. For once, he had a few people on his side. That gave him enough support to match Odette's power.

"I'm only sayin' what everyone is thinkin'. Here's our Jake, lying dead out on the beach, while the chief's off gallivantin' with the voodoo queen. Mary Gleason saw them headin' out of town last night in his truck. Weren't no official business, neither."

The gazes turned my way could have burned holes into cement.

I looked at Arnold James, my heart beating like thunder in my ears. "What I do in my private life is my business. Chief Burke was off duty at the time and not in any way shirking his responsibilities."

Arnold fixed me with a sharp look. "He oughta be on the job twenty-four hours a day until this murderer is caught. Now one of his own men is dead. One of the best men in town." Arnold sniffed a little, then rubbed his nose on his sleeve.

Despite his verbal attack, compassion welled in me. I reached out and put my hand on Arnold's shoulder. "He grew up with your boys, didn't he? Just like I did. I loved him, too, Arnold."

Arnold pulled his shoulder away, but his energy shifted to a more manageable level.

I glanced at Odette. Her pale blue eyes told me everything I needed to know. There was nothing she could do now to repair the damage to my reputation. Only I could do that. I would have to start all over again.

If I wanted to.

Did I?

"Let me clear some of these plates." I chose action over thought for now.

The others handed me their plates. I felt the gazes of the women, curious and examining. A few of the men eyed me with a certain glint, as if the salacious news of my out-of-town trip with the chief made me a "loose woman".

Anger shot through me. I was sick of this. Sick of the constant judgment and sense of being evaluated every waking moment. And yet these were my people. My neighbors, my friends, my tribe. I knew I'd do what I had to in order to protect them, even if some of them didn't deserve it. It was the MacPherson way, right or wrong.

I walked to the kitchen with the plates. The breakfast rush was almost over. Soon it would be time for the lunch crowd. I set the plates in the sink and opened the cabinet for the change of menus. Today's lunch special was catfish. Sarabeth was already hard at work, preparing her world-famous catfish coating at the center prep island.

"The sharks smell blood, don't they?"

I stopped and leaned on the counter next to her. "How could you tell?"

"You've got bite marks all over you, *cherie*." She tossed the bread coating in the mixing bowl with her gloved hands.

I sighed, dejected. "The word's gone out. I might

as well get a scarlet 'S' for 'slut' and pin it to my t-shirt. That would make them happy."

"It's not their fault. They're still asleep inside. They don't know anything beyond what they can see, hear, smell, taste, and touch. They don't know what else is out there, beyond the boundaries of this town and their own minds. You do."

She fixed me with a stare until I looked at her directly. "You're different, Selene. Always have been. With the day comes the night. This is it, baby girl. The dark. But you know your way out. You've got the light inside you."

"I don't know if that's enough." If I wasn't careful, I could lose my business. I depended on customers to make it work. The locals were everything once the tourist season ended. If I lost the business, I could lose the house when the taxes weren't paid. I could lose everything I held dear, all that was mine.

But I could also lose Adrian. Before I even had a chance to find out if I wanted him.

*****

The night drew near, casting its purple cape over the sea. I sat down on one of the dunes, the wind whipping my broomstick skirt around my bare feet. I closed my eyes and opened my heart.

"Jake. If you're here, let me help you. Let me guide you to the Otherworld."

I waited, listening with my inner senses, watching with my inner eyes. Nothing. All that surrounded me was the wind, the sea spray, and loneliness.

I opened my eyes, sighing at my failure to give

aid to someone who had meant so much to my young heart. I knew I'd be breaking curfew, and that it was probably dangerous to be on the beach at nightfall. Even this beach, where I'd grown up and spent my whole life. Yet I felt I owed this to him, for the sake of old times.

I listened again, open to any indication that he had heard me. Perhaps he'd already crossed over. Murder victims were at times trapped for a few days in the world they'd known, trying to make sense out of the sudden, unexpected change in their existence. But it didn't always happen that way. Maybe Jake had been one of the lucky ones.

"Where is it?" I heard a voice say, so close to my ear it could have been a breath of wind. But it sounded like Jake.

I closed my eyes again, straining to hear. "Where is what?"

"Knife. Broken. Piece left."

"Knife? You mean the murder weapon? Show me where to look." I climbed to my feet.

"Big one. Palm tree. On top."

I glanced around me, looking for a palm tree. There weren't that many on this stretch of beach. Then I spied it, about twenty yards away. A lone palm tree at the pinnacle of a huge sand dune that led to the road.

I ran down the beach as fast as I could, before the fading light made vision impossible. The sand dune piled high over my head, but I mounted it.

Then I stopped. What if by walking on the loose sand, I caused the knife to slip into the dune, lost for good? I backed away, my mind lost in the various considerations.

I hit a solid wall of muscle.

I spun around, screaming as loudly as I could. Then I took a swing at whatever loomed over me. If it wanted to kill me, I wouldn't make it easy.

The dark figure wrestled with me before I landed a lucky shot in his solar plexus with my fist. His breath rushed out in a whoosh as he landed on his knees. I ran, faster than I knew I could fly.

The figure dragged in a deep breath, then cried out, "Selene!"

I stopped, my skirt swirling around my legs. I looked back, leaning forward as I sucked a deep breath into my lungs. The thing knew my name?

"It's me." The figure cried out, still on its knees in the sand.

Adrian.

Damn him.

Chapter Ten

"What the hell are you doing here?"

Adrian rubbed his upper stomach as he stood. "I should ask you the same question. Damn, you pack a wallop."

"Quit sneaking up on me."

He walked toward me, then looked down from his considerable height. "If you wouldn't keep acting so suspicious, maybe you wouldn't have to worry about people sneaking up on you."

Did he think he could bully me? He had no idea. I met his gaze head-on. "This is a public beach. I have every right to be here."

"It's also almost curfew, and a recently cleared crime scene. Spill it. What are you doing here alone? Offering yourself as the next victim?"

A sharp retort slid down the barrel of my verbal gun, but one look into his eyes stilled my anger.

He was the walking wounded.

"No. I'm not trying to do that. I came to help Jake."

He glanced away from me toward the sea and watched the waves pull out at low tide. I sensed how uncomfortable my world still made him, even though he no longer fought its reality.

He looked back at me, his mouth twisted as if in thought. "And did you?"

"He's still here. He told me to look in this dune. The killer must have crossed this way. Jake says there's a part of the murder weapon at the top."

Adrian looked up at the dune towering over our

heads. "You're kidding. We need to get my cell phone and call Lieutenant Andrews."

"Your cell phone? Why not use the police radio?"

He swung his gaze to me, his mouth tight. "That's why I came looking for you. To tell you the news. The mayor of Fort Bedford has seen fit to cancel my contract. I'm out, Selene. Fired."

"How could they do that? Can't you fight it?"

He shook his head. "I should have known better. This was all wrong. I just wanted out of Chicago. Away from the cold, the snow —"

"The memories."

"Yeah. Thought I'd go south and start a new life. That's what I get for trying, huh? Anyway, just wanted you to know. I'll call Andrews, get the guys out here. Although I'm not sure how I'm going to explain the source of this information." He chuckled, his laughter harsh with frustration.

"Tell him to talk to me. I'm the source. At this point, we might as well come clean. We're the talk of the town anyway."

He put his hands in his pockets. "Yeah, aren't we? I've never lived in a small town, with this kind of social scrutiny and clannish behavior. I don't know how you survive it."

"It has its advantages as well as its drawbacks. Just like anything else, I guess." Wasn't that the truth.

I lifted my head and forced a smile for his benefit. "Let's go get that cell phone. Give the people something to really talk about."

"You're on."

We walked down the beach toward his parked truck as the sun set. He didn't take my hand or make any effort to touch me. But he was there. The two of us, against the world. It was a start.

*****

Within the hour, the tranquil beach transformed into a full-out investigation. Cars, men, lights, equipment. The beach crawled with activity.

Adrian sat by my side on a cluster of rocks as the investigators descended upon us.

"So you say the murder victim talked to you? In a dream?" The young, pencil-necked state investigator stood over me, a white pad in his hand as he scribbled God-knows-what.

"No. It's rather hard to explain. I shift consciousness and open myself to the Otherworld. The world of spirit that exists alongside this world. Once I do that, I can contact those who have crossed over."

The investigator cocked an eyebrow and glanced at me over his pad. "Otherworld, huh? You some kind of sixth sense person? You know, 'you see dead people'?"

I held back the urge to roll my eyes. "Yes. Precisely. I see dead people. Hear them, too."

"Okay. Well, I'd appreciate your not leaving the area until we're finished with our investigation." He slapped the pad shut, dismissing me.

"Not a problem. We're not going anywhere." Adrian took my hand.

The investigator glanced at us, then nodded. "Sit tight. We'll be back with you in a while."

"I'll bet you will." Adrian watched the younger man as he walked away. "Arrogant jerk."

"Professional rivalry talking?" I gave his hand a little squeeze.

"No, just an honest observation." His hand relaxed around mine at little.

I leaned closer. "Thank you for staying with me. I wouldn't want to be alone in this."

He looked away, his eyes on the men down the beach. "I could hardly leave. I'm the one who called the dogs."

"Well, thanks anyway." His impersonal reply stung.

He must have noticed my reaction. "Hey." He slid a finger under my chin as he turned my face to his. "Either way, I wouldn't leave you alone. Not when you need me."

Did I need him? I didn't want to. I smiled, deciding no response was better than any comment I could make. It was all too confusing, too raw, too fresh.

He didn't seem to notice. He slipped an arm around my waist, still holding my hand as we watched the investigators sift through the sand.

"I'm sorry about last night. It's hard to talk about it. The accident."

My caution fell away at his gentle words. "I know. But I'm glad you did."

"Hey, you never kept your end of the bargain."

"Oh? What do you mean?"

"You never told me your secret. The hardest one to hold inside."

I laid my head on his shoulder. "I guess I'll have to, huh? Fair is fair."

"Only if you want to." His lips grazed my

forehead, easing my nerves.

"Well, I guess it would be the real reason why Jason said he left me. It wasn't his girlfriend. She was the symptom, not the cause."

"Go on."

I turned my head and gazed out at the sea. "Jason and I married young, right out of high school. He was pretty much the only boy in town brave enough to take on one of the MacPhersons. There used to be a rumor that any man who married one of us would grow warts all over his body, particularly their-well, you know."

"That's crazy. Didn't they know that?"

I laughed at the memory. "You don't know the Deep South, Adrian. A lot of old country traditions still exist down here, along with the superstitions and fears that grow alongside them. For some of these boys, the warts story made perfect sense."

I patted his hand as he quirked an eyebrow at me. "Anyway, I realize now one reason why I was so alluring to Jason. He was the preacher's son. Talk about the ultimate rebellion. Angel boy romances the witch girl. Probably made his father apoplectic. Before we knew it, we were swept up in the thrill of love, the idea of passion. As soon as we graduated, he asked me to marry him. And I did, a few days after the commencement ceremony. I guess I was rebelling, too. My rebellion was to grab onto the respect and validation being Jason's wife would give me. I guess we came at each other with cross-purposes, right from the start."

I sighed, wishing I hadn't started this sharing game. "Not long after we were married, I found out I was pregnant. When I was eight months along, my parents died in an airplane crash on the way home from one of Daddy's trials. Daddy was a lawyer, a partner with Mr. McCarty. In a flash, two eighteen-year-olds had a baby and a nine-year-old orphan to raise. It was a disaster in the making."

"What happened?"

I shifted in his embrace, but he held me close. "There wasn't much choice. Raising Izzy and Steph became my primary focus. I took care of the girls during the day, then worked at night to help bring in the money we needed, now that two mouths to feed became four. Jason's pay as assistant manager at the hardware store wasn't enough."

I took a shuddering breath as the memories of our fights over money, control, the kids, echoed in my mind. "Then we had Lissa, and it became even more difficult. But we did our best. I thought we were as happy as we could be, taking everything into account. I thought he understood if we could just hold on, things would get better. But he didn't."

"Did you find them in your bed?"

I turned around in his arms. "How did you know?"

"I didn't know." His brows knit together in a frown. "I saw a picture of it flash in my head, like a slide in a projector. Is that how it works for you?"

I settled back in his embrace, amazed. "Yes, sometimes. Maybe you have some latent ability, Adrian."

"Great. That's the last thing I need to deal with now." I sensed his withdrawal at the thought of his own ability. Then he shook it off and refocused. "Go on. What happened when you confronted them?"

"They freaked out. He tried to deny everything. Pretty hard to do when your girlfriend is sitting there naked as the day she was born." I snorted at the thought. "His girlfriend. She worked at the store with him as a cashier. Nineteen years old. One of those skinny, rose-tattooed, strawberry-blonde-from-a-bottle types. It didn't take long for Jason to choose her over me. They took off to New York five years ago, as soon as the divorce papers were filed. He never looked back. I think he called the girls twice in five years."

"What about child support?"

"He changes jobs, uses fake Social Security numbers. No one can track him long enough to garnish his wages. I finally gave up. I couldn't afford to keep chasing him. I had the girls and Izzy to deal with. So I pulled myself together and just did it."

Adrian chuckled, then laid his cheek against my hair. "Is this the secret? That you can do anything you set your mind to? I already had that one figured out."

"No, that's not it. The secret is, Jason said I'd become a bore. I worked too much, I didn't spend enough time focused on him, I'd lost my sex appeal. I'd worked hard to become what he said he wanted-a good wife, a good partner, a good mother. Then when I finally accomplished it, he dumped me for becoming what he'd asked. He tossed in a parting shot about being a 'lousy lay' for good measure. Funny, isn't it, in view of what everyone thinks of me? The exotic, mysterious 'voodoo queen'. But he was probably right."

I looked away, embarrassed. Yet somehow with Adrian, I knew I could say the words and not die inside.

"He lied, Selene. Men say crap like that so you'll take all the blame on yourself and they can get away scot-free. Don't you believe it."

I stroked the back of our joined hands in my lap. "I always did believe it. Until last night, with you."

He made a sound, deep in his chest, and then put both arms around me.

"I'm glad."

A cool breeze swept over us, different from the wind from the ocean. I picked up the scent of the aftershave I'd smelled earlier that evening and smiled. It was Jake's. He'd always worn the same brand, ever since Mille O'Connor told him it smelled sexy back in 1992.

"Loved you." Jake's voice hummed with energy inside my mind, but it was weakening.

I closed my eyes and connected, tears rushing forward. "I loved you, too. I'm sorry about the spell I cast. The only love worth having is the kind that's freely given."

"Don't hold back." The voice grew distant. He was crossing, exiting this plane of existence.

I sent out a blessing as his spirit took its leave.

"Hey, MacPherson. Burke."

I jerked free of the connection, caught for a moment between this world and the next.

"You two, come with me." The investigator with the movie quote fixation motioned to us with his hand.

Adrian pulled me to my feet. I had a hard time

standing. I was still caught in-between the worlds. Jake's spirit and the investigator's interruption played havoc with my equilibrium.

"You okay?" Adrian looked into my eyes.

I glanced up at him, dragging in a deep breath. "I will be. C'mon, let's see what they've found."

We walked behind the investigator to the edge of the dune, where another pair of officers advanced toward us.

"Well, Ms. MacPherson, I'd have to give your psychic abilities an A plus." The older blue-suited officer lifted a small baggie in front of our faces.

I leaned forward to see what it was and gasped. One side of the shank of a knife. A black-handled knife. The same as I'd seen in my first vision.

"We're taking this in for tests. Burke, I've been advised about the change in your status. Bad break. Don't think you deserved it."

"Thank you, sir." Adrian stood a bit taller.

"I'd like to ask both of you to make yourselves available to us as we continue this investigation."

"We will."

I couldn't tear my gaze away from the partial knife shank in the officer's hand. Jake was a better cop in death than he was in life. He'd helped solve his own murder.

"If you need us, you can call my cell phone or the home phone at Ms. MacPherson's."

"Will do. Good work, you two." With that, the officer turned away and rejoined his group.

I glanced at Adrian, still dizzy from the night's events.

"Now what?"

"Now we go home. And we wait."

*****

Adrian and I walked through the back door to a chaotic scene that was natural to me. But to him? I didn't know.

"Mama, Steph won't be quiet so I can finish my summer math work."

Steph turned to Lissa and put her hands on her hips. "I'm not doing anything to you. Why don't you grow up, you big baby. Always calling 'mama, mama, mama'."

"Do not!" Lissa's lower lip stuck out farther than the bumper on my car and her expression turned surly. "Mama said I had to do this extra math work so I wouldn't forget how to do it next year. You won't turn off your stupid music so I can study."

"I live in this house, too. No one ever lets me do anything around here."

"Enough!" I yelled over the din.

I glanced at Adrian, wondering what he thought. He leaned against the back door, a hand over his mouth. If he thought this was amusing, he ought to be here at allowance distribution time.

I turned back toward the girls. "Steph, you may play your music as loudly as you want, as long as it doesn't disturb the other people who also live in this house."

Steph's expression showed her frustration at having her own words turned back on her, but she wisely crossed her arms and nodded.

"As for you, Lissa, why don't you bring your books down here and work at the kitchen table? It would mean more room for you and it's quieter. If you need help, I'm here."

"Okay." Lissa gave Steph a sharp look. She hated losing any ground to her sister. It was a never-ending battle.

"Say hello to Mr. Burke." I hoped the girls could cease-fire long enough to remember their manners.

"Hi, Mr. Burke. Want to see my worm collection? You didn't get to see it the other day."

He smiled. "Maybe later."

"Steph, say hello." I lifted my eyebrow at her.

Steph stood with her hands behind her back, her energy glum and defiant. "H'Lo."

Apparently our talk earlier in the day had little effect on her attitude. I sighed, wondering why I couldn't find the right words.

"It's good to see you again." Adrian gave her his warmest smile, but it seemed to only displease her more.

"I'm going to my room." Steph grabbed a can of soda from the kitchen table.

"I'm gonna get my books. Be right back." Lissa's happiness at Adrian's presence lifted the energy.

My daughters. A walking dichotomy.

"Sorry about that." I tossed my keys on top of the dishwasher. "They can be a handful."

"That's okay. They get it from their mother."

I slugged him in the arm and he laughed. "Watch it, Burke. I'm the voodoo queen around here. I might cast a spell on you."

He moved closer, his body brushing mine. "Haven't you already?"

I closed my eyes when his chest grazed the front

of my t-shirt, rousing a quick, tingling sensation in my breasts. Instantly my blood warmed. I smoothed his shirt around his waist, letting my hands dip lower toward the back pockets of his jeans. He threaded his fingers into to my hair as I lifted my face to his.

Lissa ran into the kitchen, her tennis-shoed feet slapping the wood floor. "Mama, look at all the work I've finished."

I pulled away from Adrian and mouthed an apology to him, but he only smiled and shook his head, then whispered in my ear.

"Later."

Oh, yes.

"Come look, Mama." Lissa spread her work across the table.

Adrian approached from behind as I looked over her figures. She'd made a lot of progress. Her teacher had suggested she do special work on mathematics over the summer to boost her grades next fall. Unfortunately for Lissa, she'd inherited my ineptitude for numbers along with the family gift. It took every ounce of my limited ability to keep the household and business ledgers from becoming a horrific mess.

"This is great, baby girl. I'm so proud of you." I smoothed her hair as she beamed from my praise.

Adrian nodded and encouraged her as she showed him her neat, orderly columns of numbers. I watched them for a moment, then turned away as a sharp jab of fury struck.

He followed me when I walked to the refrigerator and pulled out a pitcher of tea. I poured a glass and took a long swallow.

"What's the matter?" He leaned on the counter

beside me.

"It's just-sometimes I hate Jason so much for leaving me. But I mostly hate him for what he took away from the girls. No father. No male to look up to, no man to give them any idea what men should be. All they have is his ghost. That, and abandonment. Damn him." I took another drink, forcing myself to calm down.

"You can't change the past, Selene. But look at it this way. He left gold for brass. He's the biggest loser. The girls still have you."

I took a third sip to cover the sudden urge to cry. Adrian was like a healing balm to my spirit. I didn't want to like him so much. I hoped I could cover my reaction. "So, what do you think so far about the murders?"

He cocked his head at my sudden change in conversation and his expression grew serious. "At this point, the killings seem targeted at tall, dark-haired males. Ages thirty and up. Slim builds. Usually males well known to the women around here, except in the case of the tourist, but even he was seen with a woman just before he went missing. The involvement of the men with the women may be a part of the killer's trigger. I don't know."

He rubbed his face, the exhaustion of the past few days coloring the hollows under his eyes. "The killer seems to enjoy stalking the men. The wounds are always in the back, a sneak attack. The department has determined that the murderer has to be a man, due to the depth of the wounds, the angle, and the force involved. Which, by the way, puts your sister in the clear. Not that she was ever a serious suspect in my mind. I was just doing my job, Selene. I hope you understand that. I know for a fact that the state police are no longer considering her as a possible."

"I do understand. Thank you, Adrian." Somewhere inside me, a small door of anxiety finally closed. One, at least.

He nodded. "I wish we had more to go on. We-I mean, they have a partial footprint from the woods at the second murder, thanks to you. They also have a portion of the murder weapon now. But that's all the material evidence we have."

I took another sip of tea, focusing on the clues. "What about the missing fingers? That's the part I don't understand."

"Same here. Why fingers? Why two at a time? Is the killer keeping them? Why do it at all? If that's his message, no one is getting the point."

Our gaze drifted back to Lissa, hard at work. I longed for her innocence, the joyful way she took to life. Maybe I hadn't messed up completely as a parent.

She dropped her pencil and sighed, then bent over her paper and rubbed the eraser over her error. Holding up her small, stubby hands, she started to count.

"One, two, three, four..." Lissa's high voice sang out.

I wondered if she was too old to still be using her fingers. I made a mental note to ask her teacher in September.

"Five, six, seven, eight..."

Adrian suddenly stiffened beside me, his mouth hanging open.

"Nine, ten."

"That's it." Adrian grasped my arm.

"What's it?"

He leaned forward and kissed me, then strode out the back door.

"Where are you going?" I called as he walked down the steps toward the driveway.

"Back to the beach. I know why the killer is taking the fingers."

"You do? How?"

"Lissa told me."

I closed the door behind me and put my hands on my hips. "What are you saying?"

He looked back at me. "It's not just a malicious act, Selene. It's a countdown."

I fell against the railing behind me as the impact of his words hit home. First two. Then four. Now six. A countdown, by twos. Building up to ten? And then what?

"Hurry, Adrian." A cold blanket of dread settled, submerging me in its claustrophobic embrace.

"I'll be back." He rushed to his truck.

I went into the house and locked the door tight.

Chapter Eleven

I sat at the kitchen table with only a single candle lit and shuffled the tarot deck.

The girls had gone to sleep much earlier. I'd spent time at the table that night holding hands with Izzy, comforting her and listening to her experiences with the Nelsons. After so much reluctance on their part about their son dating one of "us", they'd come to accept and embrace her. I was glad, for her sake.

Sean's funeral was scheduled for tomorrow afternoon. There would be more than one funeral to attend this week, for everyone in Fort Bedford. I sighed, burdened by the measure of so much loss.

I decided to do a past, present, and future spread with the cards, to get a read on the energies Adrian and I faced. I turned the first card, signifying the Past. The Seven of Cups. Illusions. I frowned at that one. Was the killer's intent not based on reality, but on what he perceived? I turned the second card, indicating the Present. The Moon. Deception. I held the card and examined the image. Two dogs howled at a shimmering full moon overhead. This told me the murders were more than what meets the eye. Were we on track to discovering the right clues, or were we already hopelessly off course? I didn't want to think what might happen if that were the case. The last card was the future card. I turned it, then froze as the red-robed image of Death met my gaze, the white rose beside it indicative of endings. I shuffled the cards back into the deck, a cold shiver in my bones. *Please don't let us be too late. We can still stop this. The energies aren't set in stone.*

I heard Adrian's truck door slam outside. I looked down at the deck in my hands, then turned another card. The Lovers, again. I laid the image on top of the stack and stared at it. Was I ready to become lovers with Adrian? I didn't know.

He tapped lightly on the back door. I rose from the table and unlocked the bolt.

"Did they listen to you?" I kept my voice low, even though the household had already fallen asleep.

He kissed my cheek, then took a seat at the table. He glanced at the candle and the tarot deck. "Working a little voodoo for me?"

I shook my head. "Very funny. I use tarot to help me direct my natural gifts. Besides, a little extra information won't hurt." I sat next to him at the table, facing the deep purple candle I'd lit to aid me in my concentration. The flame on the candle flickered and leapt. Spirits present. I prayed they were benevolent.

"Tell me," I reached out to take his hand.

"I went to Lieutenant Andrews. He agreed my theory made sense. We're stepping up our efforts. We need to focus harder on the information we've gathered, form a better plan of attack, and get this perp captured." He shook his head. "Damn. I keep doing that. They, not we. I'm not a part of this anymore."

I leaned forward on the table. "You're wrong. We're both a part of this, up to our eyeballs. We have to be careful. The killer saw us. He knows we're aware of information we've made known to the police. He might decide to do something about it. In case you haven't noticed, you're a tall, slim, dark-haired male in his thirties. Seen about town with a woman. Just what the killer is apparently hunting."

His eyes widened for a moment. "That didn't cross my mind. I was focused on the investigation."

I squeezed his hand. Then I interrupted him. "You were the cop at work. But Jake's death proves no one is safe, Adrian. Not even you."

"I guess I'll need a keeper then, so I'll stay out of trouble." He smiled his little half grin, then ran a finger down the back of my hand. "Know any volunteers who might want to take on the task?"

I glanced at the deck of cards. The Lovers beckoned, reminding me of pleasures and caresses I'd thought would never be mine again. I gazed into the dancing flame, then whispered a prayer. "Watch over us, dear friends, all through the night." Then I leaned forward and blew out the candle. Moonlight filled the kitchen with its gentle, numinous glow.

I turned to Adrian and looked into his eyes. "I volunteer."

He stood next to me, and then pulled me to my feet. "Are you sure? It's a challenging job."

I leaned forward and kissed his chest through the cotton of his shirt. His quick, indrawn breath at my touch told me the answer.

"I think I'm woman enough."

*****

We crept up the stairs and down the hall to my room. Doubt warred inside me, shaking my resolve. How could I bring him into my house, into my bed? Shouldn't we go to a motel off the highway? What if the girls or Izzy saw us? We shouldn't be doing this.

I knew I should listen to my brain and put an end to it, but my heart and my body could no longer wait. I realized I wanted him here. In this house, where I'd grown up, laughed, cried, worked. Where I felt the strongest, the safest, the most real. I wanted to give that to him. To myself.

I opened the door and led him inside, then closed it and pressed the lock. I gazed up at him in the midst of the shadows. Moonlight shone through the windows on either side of my bed, casting twin shafts of soft, white light onto the floor. The room smelled faintly of the lavender and sandalwood incense I'd burned earlier in the day. What was calming and soothing in the light turned seductive and powerful in the dark. The magical effects of the perfumed oils weaved their way around us, caressing and coaxing.

Adrian stepped closer, then put his arms around me.

"I'm afraid." I slid my hands over the hard, rippled planes of his stomach. "It's been five years since the last time I-."

He raised a finger to my lips. "You don't have to say it. This is the first time for me, too, since then."

I smiled, a bit of relief taking the edge off my fear. "Really?"

He chuckled. "I may not remember how. You'll have to remind me."

I laughed, then covered my mouth with my hand. "I'll bet you'll figure it out as we go along."

He bent down and lifted me against him, my feet dangling at his shins. "You're all the inspiration I need."

Then he kissed me, his lips hot and needy. I

returned the kiss, letting go of my inhibitions and questions. I didn't want solutions tonight.

I wanted him.

He carried me to the bed, then laid me on the covers, following me with his body. I ran my hands over the hard muscles of his back and up into his hair as he kissed my neck. Then he traveled down, his lips whispering across the mounds of my breasts to the hollow of my belly. He pressed his face into the warm heat beneath my skirt. I almost cried out at the intimate pleasure.

He lifted his body with his arms, his breath fast and heavy. "I wanted to take this slow, but I don't know if I can. I want you, Selene. I have to see you, now." Untying the sash of my skirt, he pulled away the fabric and tossed it onto the floor. He did the same with my t-shirt, leaving me clad in only a pair of white bikinis and a bit of lace.

"Oh, God." He looked down at me as if I was the most beautiful woman in the world.

I reached for his buckle, undoing the tongue of his belt with shaking fingers. He rose and stood motionless for me next to the bed, as if he was afraid to move and shatter the moment. His hands gently squeezed my shoulders as I eased his jeans from his long, muscular legs. I could see how much he wanted me. It filled me with feminine power, a sense of self I'd never known. I lifted my hands to reach under his shirt, hungry for more.

He jumped back when my fingers touched the scars.

I stood, the moonlight from the window bathing us in its enchantment. A look of pain and fear moved over his features as he began to turn away. I shook my head, refusing to let him go.

Slowly I unbuttoned his shirt, one by one. I undid the cuffs to caress the scar on the back of his right hand. He made a strangled sound in his throat, but remained still. Finally I spread the shirt open and pushed it over his shoulders.

The burn scars coursed their way up his right arm and down the length of his side, finally ending near his belly button. The tight, shiny skin contrasted with the smooth, muscular tone of the rest of his body. I thought then of the pain and suffering he'd endured, the months of therapy, the fear of never recovering. The loss of Madelyn, the unjust blame he put on himself.

His wounds had healed. Not his heart. I ran my fingers gently over the edge of his scars. He drew in a breath, his rib cage pressing toward me. His face reflected all the fear and shame I knew he held inside.

His voice trembled. "I'm sorry. I'm not-"

A tear slipped from my lashes as I did the only thing I could to think of, to tell him how I felt. I pressed my lips to the center of the scars.

A harsh gasp came from deep inside him. He reached down and burrowed his hands in my hair, his lips working to hold back his emotion.

I lifted my head. "You're beautiful to me, Adrian. In every way."

He kissed me, harder this time, unleashing everything within him. I felt possessed, encircled, yet potent in my womanhood. I threw my arms around him and returned the kiss with all the emotion I'd kept locked away for so long. His hands moved over my skin, sweeping away the bra and panties before I realized it. He knelt in front of me, his tongue laving the rise of my lower belly as he kissed and nipped at the skin.

Finally he dipped lower into the wet core of my desire. I cried out and dug my fingers into his hair, holding on for balance as I pressed him closer. "Don't stop."

I felt the answer of his laughter against my flesh as he delved deeper, further. The rapture of it shook my senses as my body throbbed from the power of his touch. I was giving, yet taking. I opened my legs wider, wanting more. He gladly obliged.

He flipped me onto my back, then bent down to get something out of the pocket of his discarded jeans.

"Came prepared?" I couldn't help but smile.

"Came hoping." He gave me a devilish grin as he ripped open the green foil package and pulled out the condom. I watched as he rolled the thin sheath onto his penis, his face eager with excitement. The sight of him was heady, dizzying.

He returned to me. I opened my arms to him, ready to take him inside me. I wanted him to fill me and never let me go. I wanted to feel this joy forever.

He plunged deep, igniting me with yearning for him. I wrapped my legs around him, riding him as much as he rode me. Sweat dripped from his brow, mingling with the tiny trickles that slid from my skin. Higher and higher, he took me to a paradise of light, sound, and pounding, blinding pleasure. At last the world exploded around me, shattering into a shower of bright, shimmering ecstasy.

He held me tight as his own passion burst free.

His long, shuddered moan of completion filled me with a bliss I hadn't thought possible. I drew him down, cradling his head against my neck as we struggled to catch our breath.

I would never be the same.

*****

I opened my eyes as the alarm buzzed in my ear, shocking me out of a dream I didn't want to end. Delicious, decadent. Adrian in all his glory, while I-

The alarm abruptly shut off.

"Good morning." A kiss brushed my cheek.

I bolted upright in bed and realized I was naked. "Adrian, you didn't go home last night."

He rolled onto his side, his lazy grin aglow in the faint moonlight. "That's right. You begged me to stay, remember?"

Oh, yes. I did. I'd begged him for a lot of things.

He'd delivered, on each and every one of them.

A torrent of hot embarrassment swept over me as I recalled each detail. I couldn't believe it. I should turn in that scarlet "S" for slut and get an "I" for insatiable. "You have to leave, before anyone sees you." I jumped out of bed, pulling the sheet with me.

"Why? It's four-thirty in the morning. Only you and the owls are up at this hour. Come back to bed. I'll make it worth your while." He pulled on the tail of my sheet.

I glanced back at him sprawled naked in my bed. He was masculine and dark against the white lace pillowcases. Worth my while? I tugged at the sheet, aware of the soreness in my muscles. If I didn't get him out of here, I was never going to walk again. It wasn't my fault. I didn't normally bend and twist my body into that many positions in the space of an hour. Oh God. "I mean it. You have to leave. I don't want my girls to catch a naked man in the hallway."

He grinned. "They won't. I promise I'll have pants on."

I growled, which seemed to only amuse him further. "I have to go to work. Get up, right now." I gave the sheet one last jerk. "I'm sorry, Adrian. I don't want anyone to know this about us."

"Oh. I understand." He dropped the sheet, then rolled away and grabbed his jeans from the floor. He shoved his feet into the legs, and then stood from the bed.

I couldn't help but watch as the blue denim slid over his tight, firm bottom. What a man.

He turned to me, his expression sober as he shrugged on his shirt.

I suddenly realized the mess I'd created. "Adrian, it's not that I'm ashamed of us. It's just, well, complicated."

He shook his head, his focus on buttoning his shirt. "Hey, you don't have to explain. I get it. It was fun, right? Just sex."

"You don't understand-"

"I'll see you later. The funeral is at three o'clock. I'll be there."

I sighed. There was no sense arguing with him in his present mood. "All right. I'll see you there."

He pulled on his shoes. He paused. Finally he kissed me briefly on the top of my head and without another word, left the room.

So much for romantic goodbyes.

I sat down on the bed, the sheet still wrapped around my breasts. Still scented with the fragrance of our lovemaking.

Congratulations, Selene. Feel safer now?

*****

The bells of the church tolled with a long, low gong as the girls and I escorted Izzy to a pew in the front row. The little Methodist chapel was filled to overflowing. My regular customers, friends, and local townspeople packed tight into every available seat. The heat level climbed as one lone air conditioner chugged away from a window over the choir loft.

Izzy held together pretty well, considering the stress. Several men and women her age embraced her and expressed their condolences. I wondered how many of them had begun as Sean's friends, but were now hers. Being with Sean had given her a network of companionship, at least among the twenty-somethings in town. I hoped it lasted beyond the funeral. She deserved real friendship.

I looked over my left shoulder, scanning the crowd for Adrian. I hated how we'd left it that morning. Just sex? He had no idea how much being with him had meant to me. How much he had come to mean to me, in only four days.

I had to convince him.

I turned to the right, then caught sight of Richard Swann and Janell, their heads together in whispered conversation. Immediately, a sense of confusion sank its teeth into my awareness. A dark, nauseous wave engulfed me. It had to be the heat. I rose from my seat and excused myself, then rushed outside.

My head cleared as I drew in a deep, cleansing breath. The white clapboard church felt cool against my back. I closed my eyes.

"Selene? Are you all right?"

Adrian stood over me, dressed in a light gray suit. My heart leapt at the sight of him.

"I'm okay. The heat got to me. That's all. I'm glad to see you, Adrian. I'm sorry about this morning. Will you let me explain?"

He stood straight and glanced back into the church. "No need. Come on, the minister is starting the service."

I ground my teeth at his avoidance. If I had to wrestle him to the ground, I'd make him listen to me. But not now. Not here.

We stood at the back of the church as the minister conducted the service. The burial took place in the little cemetery behind the chapel, beneath a cluster of tall pines. Short, simple, yet lovely.

"It's the way he would have wanted it." Izzy led us to the car afterward. "He wasn't a fancy man. He was just Sean."

I hugged her as she wrapped her arms tight around me.

"I love you, Isuelt MacPherson." How I wished I could erase every pain, every sorrow, from those I loved. But I couldn't even do that for myself.

"I love you, too." She pulled away and wiped a tear. "I'm heading to Sean's house. His family is receiving mourners and they want me to be there. Will you come by in a while?"

I nodded. "Of course I will. Girls, do you want to ride with your Aunt Izzy?"

The girls ran to our side and each put an arm around their aunt's waist.

I nodded, touched by their open show of love. "I'll come later. I have to relieve Sarabeth and finish closing up the restaurant."

"See you later, then." Izzy dropped a kiss on Steph's brow as she hugged Lissa. They climbed into my little Toyota, waving as they drove away.

I turned and walked beneath the pines towards Sarabeth's old Buick parked down the street. The air cooled beneath the shade of the trees. It was almost pleasant, like spring. I lifted my head and tried to think of better times. Like last night, with Adrian.

The hair at the back of my neck lifted as a sudden shift in energy caught my attention. The edge of my vision shimmered like heat, giving me a sense of vertigo. I moved off the sidewalk and clutched onto a hanging tree branch for support.

Something was invading my mind, clawing at my consciousness like a crazed animal digging through a door.

"Stop it." I mentally shot back at whomever or whatever sought to occupy me. "I command you to cease."

"No." The voice in reply had an evil, shrill tone. "Too much fun. Not done yet."

"Tell me who you are." The tension in my head was unbearable as I struggled to endure the connection. Whoever this was, they were apparently unable to control what they'd tapped into. The power was in charge, not the person.

"You're mine, Selene." Sharp, brittle laughter followed the words. "Beautiful woman. So much like her. You belong to me. When I'm done, I'll take you with me."

"No!" I yelled my answer, this time out loud as well as mentally.

"You won't be able to refuse. I'll make sure of it. I'll take away your resistance. Just like this." With that, the connection snapped. The sound of it sparked through the trees like a whip of lightning. I fell to my knees on the grass as my energy drained away.

I crawled toward the trunk of a tree. Then I pulled myself to my feet. With what little awareness I could still hold onto, I stumbled to the Buick.

The killer wanted more than death now.

He wanted my life.

*****

I wasn't sure how I managed it, but I drove home in one piece. By the time I pulled into the driveway, I knew I was only moments from collapse.

"Sarabeth," I cried out, too exhausted to lift my body from the seat. "Help me."

The back door swung open and Sarabeth ran toward the car as fast as her full-figured body could carry her.

"My baby! I could feel it, I..." She stopped when she saw me and backed up a step before she recovered and opened the car door.

I rolled my head on the seat toward her, my vision blurring. "What's happening?"

"Wait right here, baby. Harlan. You, Harlan, come help me. It's Selene."

Harlan Roberts came bounding down the steps. He was still dressed in his suit from the funeral. He'd probably come to visit Sarabeth. She'd been his babysitter when we were children. He often turned to her in times of trouble. Trouble was about all we had in Fort Bedford now.

"Pick her up and carry her into the screened porch." Sarabeth directed him like a drill sergeant. I felt strong arms slip beneath my back and legs, then the sensation of flying as Harlan lifted me.

"What's the matter with me?" Was I dying? It felt as if my body was no longer my own, that I didn't have a place inside it.

"It's all right, *bebe*. Sarabeth's gonna take care of you."

Harlan laid me on the couch in the screened porch next to the back door. Daddy built the porch when we were little, to give us a place to play that would protect us from the bloodthirsty mosquitoes that took over Florida every summer. I could smell the light mildew on the cushions as Harlan lifted my head and slipped a pillow beneath me.

I opened my eyes and hazily watched Sarabeth. She brought out a dark blue bag and scattered herbs into a small cast iron cauldron. She lit a bit of charcoal and tossed it in. Within moments, clouds of white smoke billowed from the wide mouth of the pot. White Sage, I thought. I suddenly realized what she was about to do.

She began chanting, a mix of French and Cajun that I didn't understand. Harlan stepped back, a look of awe and concern on his face as he watched her. She took a long feather from the bag and began to sweep the smoke across my body. She chanted louder and took in deep breaths of the smoke, then blew them out over my head, hands, and feet.

Slowly, whatever had invaded me lifted free, as gently as the feather in Sarabeth's hand. Sage smoke was used as a natural cleansing agent. While the practice was primarily Native American, Sarabeth never turned down anything that worked. Sage was also used to chase away evil influences and negative energies. I sat up when I realized I'd been attacked. Not physically, but metaphysically, astrally. The attack had hit me with the force of a runaway train.

Sarabeth brought me a glass of water. I drank it down, even though it hit my stomach with a resounding, empty splash. I wanted to throw it up, but I lay back on the couch and breathed deeply through my nose until the nausea passed.

Finally I opened my eyes and lifted my head. Sarabeth stood over me, a frightened look on her face.

"We almost lost you. You know that, yes?"

I swallowed and tried to turn away from her words. But there was no other path for me now but the truth.

"Yes. The killer contacted me psychically. He won't stop killing, Sarabeth. Now he wants me, too."

"What do you mean, wants you?" Harlan moved to Sarabeth's side. "You mean he wants to kill you?"

I bit back a laugh. "If he wanted that, I could handle it. No. He wants me. To have me for his own. He's seen me. He's decided I'm his."

"Damn." Harlan voice was sharp with concern. "I'm getting you protection, Selene. Posting a guard outside your house and a tail to follow you."

"And how are you going to explain it? Selene got a psychic dirty phone call from the murderer? Do you know how that sounds?"

Harlan's face grew red with frustration. "They already know you helped with finding the broken part of the murder weapon. They believe in you, even if some folks in this town don't. Let me put in the request. Please."

"All right." I was too tired to fight him any longer.

He turned and kissed Sarabeth goodbye, then bent down and gave me the same. I held his face and kissed his cheek.

"I'm here for you, too." Jake's loss was our shared link now.

Harlan grinned, embarrassed by my attention. At heart he was still the same little boy who ran down the beach with me, tossing seashells and chasing sandpipers. I'd let his friendship slip from of my life after Jason left, the discomfort of the divorce driving a wedge between me and what was left of the Three Musketeers. Another little parting gift from my ex. I knew I had to refuse to let the shadow of Jason rob me of anything else.

Especially Adrian.

*****

I didn't feel comfortable telling the police what I'd experienced. I wasn't up to a long interrogation or another session with Mr. Pencil-Neck State Police about "seeing dead people". There was only one person to whom I could turn.

Adrian.

But first, I had a task to complete. It would require the greatest acting performance of my life.

"Steph, Lissa." I called up the stairs from the

landing below, as Izzy and Sarabeth stood behind me. I turned and shot them both a quick glance, then motioned to Izzy to quit wringing her hands.

She shook them, then tucked them behind her back as she pasted on a smile. Utterly unconvincing. But it was the best we could do under the circumstances.

"What is it? American Wannabe-Stars is coming on." Steph stuck her head out her door, her irritated expression clear.

"You won't miss much. Come here, I have a surprise for you."

"A surprise?" Lissa bounded down the stairs. I held my breath, always amazed that she could leap the steps two at a time and not fall on her face.

Steph walked down the stairs casually, as if she didn't care, but I saw the glint of curiosity in her eyes. It was enough to build on.

"What is it? What is it?" Lissa jumped up and down like a grasshopper.

"Great news for both of you. Aunt Izzy says it's time to take a vacation, and she's taking you with her. Guess where you're going?"

"Where?" A genuine smile lit Steph's face.

"New Orleans, to see Sarabeth's family. Won't that be great?"

"Cool," Steph replied. "Can you take us to the French Quarter to get our palms read? Can we ride on a steamboat?"

"I want crawfish." Lissa tugged on Sarabeth's skirt.

"Oh, no, child, I'm not going. I'm staying here with your Mama to help run the restaurant."

Lissa's face fell at the news.

"Oh no, you're not." I put an arm around her and pulled her hard against me. "You're going with them. I won't take no for an answer. You need some time off, and that's that."

"Yay." Lissa started jumping again. "When do we leave?"

I bent down and kissed her cheek loudly. "How soon can you pack?"

"Really? Wild." Steph rushed forward and hugged me. I held on, burying my face in her sunny hair for a moment.

"Hurry, Aunt Izzy wants to get on the road to beat traffic on IH10." I gave Lissa's bottom a playful spank. She hugged me, then ran up the stairs with her sister.

I drew in a shuddering breath and faced Izzy.

She shook her head, a small smile on her lips. "You're good, Selene. Really good. Now I know how you talked your way out of punishment when we were kids."

Sarabeth stepped closer, her fists set firmly on her hips. "Humph. You're fool crazy, too. I'm not leaving this house."

I put my hands on her shoulders and looked into her eyes. "Yes, you are. I want all of you gone until we track down this killer. I can't do this and worry about your safety. You have to trust me."

Her lower lip quivered. "I can't leave you. Your mama wouldn't want you to face this alone."

"I won't be alone. I'm calling Adrian."

"He doesn't know our practices. He can't help you the way I can." A small tear slid over her rounded cheek.

I brushed it away. "He understands more than he realizes, Sara B. It has to be like this. Go get packed. Izzy will pick you up at your house within the hour."

"I love you, baby." Sarabeth crushed me to her ample bosom.

"I love you, too." The urge to beg her to stay was overwhelming, but I held fast.

I pulled her away from me, then pressed a kiss to Izzy's cheek. "Go on, now. I need both of you to protect our girls at all cost, all right? I know what to do here."

They nodded, then turned away to prepare.

I watched them leave, a sense of loneliness covering me so deep that I thought it would bury me. Would Adrian agree to help? I wasn't completely sure, not after the way he'd acted at the church. I lifted my chin, pushing aside the anxiety threatening to overcome me. Then I walked to the old cedar chest in the corner of the room, the one we kept locked at all times. The one that belonged to Granny.

The one that held the secrets.

Chapter Twelve

"Adrian? It's me."

The cell phone connection crackled, but didn't drop off.

"Hey. Things okay over there?"

I could hear the tension in his voice. Was he trying to hold himself away from me? If so, we had to put that aside for now. There were bigger things to deal with than our relationship. If it could be called that. "I need you to come over as soon as possible. It's about the murders."

The phone line crackled again. It buzzed with an electronic hum.

"I'll be there in three minutes."

I closed my eyes and released my breath. "I'll be waiting."

I hung up the phone and glanced around the room. It looked like a magical battle zone. The contents of Granny's cedar chest spread across the dining room table in every direction. Charms, amulets, talismans, dried herbs of every kind. A bowl and pestle. Stones and crystals. And most of all, Granny's journal. Her Book of Secrets.

I picked up a clear crystal ball, as large as my hand, and peered into it. The murderer hadn't counted on the fact that when he connected with my spirit, he'd revealed his own essence. I knew what I was up against. It was far from merely human.

*****

Adrian arrived at my house in less than three

minutes. I didn't know how he did it, but I was glad to see him.

"Come in, but wait a moment." I took Granny's doubled-edged knife in my hand and cut a hole in the air around the doorway, then stood aside while he entered. Then I retraced the hole backward and chanted to restore the protective seal.

Adrian eyed the knife in my hand. "What the hell?"

"This way." I walked into the dining room and placed the knife with the other tools on the table, then turned to face him.

He walked around the table, his hand lightly touching the edge as he took in the array of artifacts. Finally he looked at me, his gaze a bit unsteady.

"Geez, Selene. You really are a witch, aren't you?"

"I prefer the term wise woman. But yes, that's what I am. The latest of a very long line." I stood a bit taller as the words slipped from my mouth. It had been many years since I'd felt true pride in my family's ways, without embarrassment or exception. I wondered how much I'd lost while I ran away from the truth. Would I be able to recapture it in time?

He picked up a bag of lavender and took a whiff of the dried purple flowers. His eyebrows lifted as he looked at me. "I smelled this scent in your room that night."

"Yes." I took the bag from him. "Lavender and Sandalwood. Sandalwood creates protection, healing, and granted wishes. Lavender brings protection, happiness, and peace. It's also supposed to attract men. The 'ladies of the evening' centuries ago used to wear it to attract customers as well as promote their services." I smiled, turning the bag over in my hands. "Not that I burned the herbs with those thoughts in mind."

"Didn't you?" He moved a step closer.

I looked at him. "Maybe."

Our gazes held, and I thought he was going to kiss me, but then he pulled away and walked to the other side of the table, his professional facade restored.

Damn.

He slipped his hands into his jeans pockets. "You said you have news about the murders."

I tried to push away the sadness his distant behavior stirred in me. I had to focus on the matter at hand. "Yes. Don't get angry, Adrian. Just listen, all right?"

He scowled, already on the defensive, but nodded in agreement.

"After Sean's funeral, the killer contacted me psychically. At least, the entity or energy that's ruling him did. It said it wasn't done yet, that it was having too much fun. And there's more."

I could tell by his stiff stance that it took all his strength to be still and listen, but he nodded.

"It said it wanted me, to have me for its own. It said something about my being 'just like her', whoever this 'her' is. I need you to help me. I don't feel comfortable going to the police with this. I need someone who's open to the full range of the metaphysical, who can deal with all that we're up against. Are you willing?"

Adrian scanned the table's contents once more,

his expression mirroring his conflict. Then his face changed, as if a veil lifted inside him. He reached down, picked up the knife, slipped it into his belt, and looked at me. "I'm your man."

A sense of vortex swept over me at his words. I suddenly had a flash of Adrian, not as he stood before me, but as he once was.

Dressed in the tartan of the MacPhersons, his hair long and wild. He knelt before the Laird of the clan.

"I am your man," Adrian said, as the Laird accepted his homage and loyalty. "None other."

The Laird placed his hand on Adrian's head and the people gathered around them cheered.

The vision lasted only a millisecond, but it was enough. I'd seen the reality. Adrian felt like home because he was home. His body held the soul of my ancestor. An ancestor who had pledged himself to the service of the MacPherson. History was repeating itself, like a spiral that never ends.

Before I had even a second to digest this fact, the phone rang. My head spun from the onslaught of so much information, but I reached over and snagged the cordless receiver.

"Hello? Yes, he's here." I handed the phone to Adrian. "It's Harlan."

Adrian took the phone from me as I crossed my arms and stood beside him. A chill tingled in my body. I moved closer to him for warmth and comfort. He put an arm around me as he talked.

"You're sure? Damn. All right. Do what the State guys tell you, Harlan. They're in charge now. Selene and I will come and see if they'll let us help. Yeah. Hang tight."

He punched the button and tossed the phone on the table behind me. Then he put both arms around me. "They've found another body."

I swallowed hard and looked up at him. "Who? Where?"

"Only about a block from here, behind the drug store. Someone you know, Selene. Mitch James, Arnold James' son."

"Oh, God." I didn't like Arnold, and Mitch had never been one of my favorites. But I mourned him now. Another soul lost to this evil. I turned my face into Adrian's shirt.

He held me tight. "It's okay to cry. I know what you feel. You think if you start crying, you might never stop. But you will. You have me now, to help you come back from the edge. Let go, baby. Let go."

And I did. I put my arms around him and cried, for all the loss, the pain, the death. He held me and didn't let go. He didn't turn away.

I wasn't alone, anymore.

*****

The moon rose over the tree line by the time we arrived at the crime scene. As in the other times, men, lights, onlookers, and activity filled the area. Four murders in four days. I wondered how any of us would ever recover from this reign of terror.

The parking lot of the drug store felt eerily similar to the bar's, giving me a sense of full circle, at least from the killer's point of view. One solitary security light hung shattered from a short wooden pole. Beneath it lay Mitch, his dark hair spread across his forehead and over his eyes. Arnold's youngest son.

The apple of his eye.

The chalk figure outlined on the asphalt around him made me think of Sean. I hoped Izzy and Sarabeth didn't catch wind of this latest turn of events, or they'd turn back toward town in a flash. That was the last thing I wanted. I needed them safe and secure, for my sake as well as theirs.

Adrian took my hand and led me to the side of Lieutenant Andrews.

Andrews looked up as we approached, then put a fist on his hip. "Figured you two would show up."

"We're here to offer our help. Nothing more. I'm here to back up Ms. MacPherson. She's prepared to attempt to tap into the energy of the crime scene, if you allow it."

Andrews drew a hand over his face. "Still not sure what I think about this. But if you can help us, MacPherson, go ahead. What do you need in order to do what you do?"

I drew in a deep breath. Then I lifted my head. "I need to get as close as I can to the victim, in order to connect with the force of the event still present in the area."

Andrews looked behind him and nodded. "I think we can do that. Cooper. Get over here."

A younger man ran to the side of the Lieutenant, his bright red hair a sharp contrast to the darkness around us.

"I need you and the crew to get this crowd back and in control. Have an escort take the family to a secured area."

Cooper nodded. "Yes, sir."

"That sufficient?"

"Yes." I smiled to show my gratitude for Andrews' openness. Maybe it was wrong to withhold the information about the killer's desire to possess me. I opened my mouth to share the information when Cooper called to Andrews for help.

A loud voice boomed above the other voices around us. "What's she doing here?"

I froze as my body recoiled from the impact of the energy flung in my direction.

Arnold James pushed through the officers, his eyes wild. "You witch! It's people like you who brought this on the town. You drew the evil here. You killed my boy!" He lunged toward me, his fists flying.

Adrian pushed me behind him as three officers grabbed hold of Arnold and held him firm.

"My boy, my boy," he moaned, as two other officers helped lead him away to a waiting patrol car. He sagged in their arms, overcome by his sorrow.

Adrian turned to me, lifting my face in his hands. "You all right? He's wrong, you know that. People say all kinds of things when they're in that kind of pain."

"I know." I lifted my trembling hands to cover his. Arnold's attack had shaken me more than I wanted to admit, but I couldn't fall apart now. "I'm okay. Let's go to work. Let's take this bastard down."

"That's my girl." He leaned down and gave me a quick kiss.

We followed Andrews until we came to Mitch's side. I crouched beside him, memories of Mitch laughing and joking as he strolled around town still alive in my mind. He lay on his stomach in the parking lot, the same as the others. Knife wounds in the back. This time, eight fingers missing. The countdown had continued and none of us had been able to stop it.

I closed my eyes and reached out to touch him. The struggle to get past my emotions and begin the process to cross the divide between this world and the Otherworld was difficult. I shut my eyes tighter, trying to force myself to calm down. Yet before I could make the jump, another energy entered the area, thick and heavy.

The killer. He entered into my mind, snaring my attention like a rabbit in a trap. I could see the bulbous cloud of muck that surrounded him as he began to show me his vision.

I saw blood pouring from Mitch's wound as the killer stood over him. I looked down and saw the knife in his hand, the missing side of the shank leaving the steel of the blade exposed. The killer turned the blade in his hands, as if measuring the new balance of the weapon.

I struggled to see more of the killer, but I couldn't get past the thick, muddy blob that surrounded him. I realized that the blob was the power of the entity, and that power was all-encompassing. It called all the shots. The man it possessed merely acquiesced and obeyed. Somewhere along the line, the man had opened himself to it. Made a karmic deal with no exit clause. The result of his choice lay dead before him.

The entity looked at me. I could sense his gaze, even though I couldn't see the murderer's face. He reached out, then touched my shoulder.

My body jerked as I swept deeper into connection. He wanted me to see something else. He pushed me, shoving me along until I stood before a small red-brick house. He pointed at the doorway with a jerk of his hand, still holding the bloody knife.

A cat sat on the welcome mat with a small, dead bird at its feet. The little claws of the bird stuck up in the air in morbid testimony. The cat washed its face contentedly then meowed. A woman appeared at the door, gasped with delight and reached down to stroke the cat. The cat leapt into her palm as it proudly presented its gift.

"Good kitty. Such a good kitty. Look what you brought me. I'm so proud of you." The woman picked up the bird and took it into the house.

The killer shoved my shoulder and turned me toward him. He lifted his left fist and held it out to me. Then he opened his fingers.

A small brown wren lay dead in his palm.

"For you," the killer hissed.

"No!" I screamed, thrust back into the mundane world with the force of a bullet. "No!"

Adrian cradled me against him. Then he shook me. "Selene!"

My eyes flew open as I grasped at his sleeves. "Get me out of here." I scrambled to my feet, shivering. "I've got to get away from other people. It's too dangerous to be near me. The killer, he-"

"What did you see?" Andrews demanded.

I struggled to pull myself together, to keep the horror of what I'd seen contained. "The same as before. The murderer wants more, he's escalating his tactics. Do what you have to do. Command a lockdown of the town, whatever. Just catch this man, before it happens again."

"What about you? Harlan Roberts put in a request for protection for your home. We're stretched too thin. Has the killer directly threatened you, MacPherson? What aren't you telling us?"

"No." I couldn't let anyone else be harmed, particularly those who couldn't grasp the deeper reality of the situation. The killer's attentions had taken a turn exclusively toward me. It was my calling to combat him and the entity driving him. "He hasn't threatened me directly."

"I'm guarding her." Adrian put his arm firmly around my shoulders.

Andrews paused, then nodded. "Stay in close contact with the State Police. We expect to hear any additional information either of you might have."

"Yes, sir."

Andrews fixed his gaze on me. "But stay out of our way unless we call you. We don't want any civilians getting hurt."

I nodded. *My sentiments exactly, Lieutenant.*

*****

I watched from under the comforter as Adrian loaded another pistol and placed it alongside the one he'd just finished. The presence of guns in the house was against my beliefs, but I didn't argue with him. All bets were off now.

"A cat wanting praise for a kill, huh? Interesting image to use."

I nodded and took another sip of my chamomile tea. "But effective. I at least know how the killer viewed this last murder. Like a present, to show me how powerful he is. I don't think the murders started out that way. That's not the energy I'm getting. But it's how they are now. Something changed, midstream. I wish I could understand it, make sense of it." I set my teacup on the side table and threaded my hands into my hair. The weariness in my body, in my mind, burdened me like an avalanche.

"We'll have to try and think like him to fully understand." Adrian rose from the coffee table to sit with me on the loveseat. He pulled me into his arms as I tossed the opposite end of the comforter over his lap.

"I don't ever want to think like him, so full of hate and malice that I no longer have a firm grasp on this world. That's what my people have fought against, all of our lives—the triumph of evil."

He chuckled and pulled me closer. "Someday you'll have to tell me all these family stories of yours."

I thought of the vision I'd been given of his soul, and its former life in the body of my ancestor. "I hope I'll get a chance."

He tipped my chin to bring my gaze to his. "You will. I guarantee it."

The unspoken fears that lay between us rose up to display their talons. I felt their presence. But looking into Adrian's eyes, I refused to allow them entry into my soul. At least for now.

I snuggled next to him, seeking his warmth and strength. "I believe you. And I promise, I won't let anything happen to you, either. I vow that, on the hearts of all the MacPhersons, alive in this world and in the Otherworld."

Adrian grinned. "Then what do I have to worry about?" He leaned down and kissed the tip of my nose.

I reached up and ran my fingers into his hair. His eyes darkened as he drew me closer beneath the comforter.

"Selene." He stroked my curls gently. "I love you. I don't know how it happened. But I know it's true."

I wasn't sure what to say. I loved him. But was I as willing as he to take the risk? Words of devotion lingered on my tongue, but my reasoning mind held them back. Too much, too soon.

"There's more. I'm sorry about the way I acted the other morning. I understand you wanted to protect your children. I want to do that, too."

"Adrian..."

"Shh. You don't have to say anything now. Just let me love you."

I put my arm around his neck and held him tight. "Yes. Love me, Adrian. Right now." I needed to feel alive, to feel safe, if only for a little while. I needed him. His vigor, his grace, his vibrant, awesome energy.

He pushed the comforter to the floor, then held me in his arms and dropped to his knees. He laid me down on the velvety softness, then rose to pull his long-sleeved white t-shirt over his head.

There was something so primal, so sexual about the movement. His chest left bare, he looked down at me as the corner of his mouth lifted in a smile. I knew then there was nothing else on Earth I wanted more than this man.

I pulled him down, not content to simply receive this time. Rolling him onto his back, I straddled him. His hands came up to clutch at my hips as my blood stirred. An ancient sense of sensual rhythm took hold. I began to rock my hips against him through his jeans, mimicking the motions of love.

He closed his eyes and his hands grasped harder at my hips, his fingers tight on my skin, urging me on. I placed my palms over his hands and closed my eyes. My head dropped back and I ground my hips into him. He groaned with pleasure. I laughed, a joyful happiness filling my heart.

"Take off your clothes." His voice was low and sultry, like the night. "I want to see all of you."

I reached down and pulled the hem of my embroidered peasant blouse over my head. I hadn't worn a bra, a nod to the heat that had settled over the town that afternoon. Adrian reached up, filling his hands with my breasts. Now it was my turn to groan.

I stood over him and undid my skirt, then let it drop to drape him like a cloud. He grinned, his hands sliding up my calves as I pulled down the thin straps of my panties. He reached up and finished the job, then lifted them to his face and breathed deeply. It was such a sexual, primitive move. I felt like a tribal priestess initiating the King, giving him the power to rule.

Adrian already ruled me.

I lay full-length against his body, enjoying the arousing friction of being naked while he remained partially clothed. He moved his hands to caress me, but I pushed them away and held them at either side of his head.

He gave me a surprised grin. "Are you going to have your way with me, dark maiden?"

"That, and then some." I leaned down to caress his face with the curls of my hair.

He moaned again, shutting his eyes as I slid the silken strands over his cheeks, then down his neck and across his chest. He reached up to touch me, but I shook my head. "No touching. You're all mine tonight."

His hands dropped beside his head and he closed his eyes. I began to trail a line of kisses from his neck, over his hard chest, then slowly down the tiny line of hair that led to more impressive sites below.

"I'm always yours, Selene."

I undid his belt buckle and moved on to the fly of his jeans. He smiled as I pulled the zipper down slowly, unleashing him. I tugged on the legs of the stiff denim. Just a couple more pulls, and-

"What was that?" Adrian's head came off the floor with a jerk.

"What was what?" I hadn't heard a thing. But then again, the sound of my heavy breathing made it hard for me to hear anything but my desire for him.

He sat up, his hands cupping my shoulders. "I'm going to check that out. Wait here."

Disappointment washed over me. "Adrian, it's probably nothing. Just the wind."

"We can't take that chance." He stood up, pulling his jeans over his hips and fixing the buckle. Then he reached for a pistol.

I shivered and wrapped myself in the comforter.

"Stay here. Don't move."

"I won't. Please be careful."

He gave me a cocky smirk. "Hey, this is my world, sweetheart. You handle the magic, I'll handle the firepower."

I knew he was trying to lighten the moment and forestall my anxiety. It was like him to think of calming me in the face of his own tension. My love for him grew as I forced myself to deliver a bright smile in return for his efforts. "You've got a deal."

He nodded, then walked out of the room along the edge of the wall, toe-to-heel so he wouldn't make any sound.

I held my breath as he disappeared into the darkness of the hallway. I hoped against hope that nothing would be outside but the brunt of the wind from the sea, or a hungry possum in search of an evening snack. I often caught the strange little creatures at night, their small, human-like hands digging through what was left of the food Lissa insisted upon leaving out for the neighborhood strays. Steph called them "giant fuzzy rats." I had to agree with her.

I stood up and pulled the comforter tight around me. The heavy, humid heat of the day had cooled into a brisk June night. The house felt clammy, like the outside of a glass of cold tea left on the table too long. I wanted to go after Adrian. I didn't like this feeling of being helpless, waiting.

A metallic crash sounded outside. I swung around, then rushed to the front window and parted the white lace curtain.

The moon colored the world with silvery-grey light as its luminosity began to wane. I looked across the property, straining my eyes to pick up any movement. Only stillness met my gaze.

I dropped the curtain. Then I did the same with the comforter. Forget this.

I bent down and gathered my clothes, then put them back on as fast as I could. Even if Adrian didn't need my help, he was going to get it.

I followed his path, walking in the same style I'd seen him adopt. The hallway seemed to stretch forever into the darkness. It never bothered me before. But tonight the darkness had a life of its own.

My back to the wall, I moved silently. Suddenly the grandfather clock began to tone midnight, the loud, resounding gong of the bell right next to my head. I almost leapt out of my skin. My heart pounded in my ears as I fell against the wall. I took a few seconds to curse the clock within an inch of its life, then took a deep breath and continued on.

There was no sign of Adrian. Where had he gone? At least inside the house, we were safe. I'd taken time to cast the protection spell from Granny's Book of Secrets on every window, every door, even the chimney of the old fireplace. Defensive amulets designed to ward off negative energies hung at each portal, reinforcing the spell.

I crossed the hall into the family kitchen. Still no sign of him. Worry began to dig into my consciousness. Something wasn't right. I closed my eyes and slid into meditation, to get a read on the energies around us.

At first I didn't pick up anything but the usual energies of the house. Mine, Izzy's, the girl's, Sarabeth's. I smiled when I picked up Adrian's, too.

His energy had mingled with ours and become a part of the blend.

I felt the power of the protective amulets, the strength of the seal around the house. I'd opened and resealed it when we'd returned home. Nothing could penetrate it but me, from the outside. The only way to break the shield was to-

Leave from the inside.

I frantically retraced the energy of the seal with my mind, searching every corner and straight line of the house for an opening. It was secured, locked down tight.

Except for the restaurant kitchen.

I threw open the connecting door and ran into the darkened dining hall. "Adrian!"

No answer.

I closed my eyes again, searching for the source of the breach. There. Down the hall, near the deserted room where Janell wanted to set up shop. I ran toward it and swung open the door.

The room was empty and silent.

Except for the open outer door, banging against the wall in the night breeze.

And Adrian's gun, abandoned on the floor.

Chapter Thirteen

I ran into the dining room and started packing. Amulets, talismans, stones, herbs. Whatever I thought I might need.

My gaze fell on the knife. Silvery steel glinted in the light from the chandelier hung over the table. The earlier image of the blade in the belt of Adrian's jeans, perched like a highlander's sword as he agreed to help me, flashed in my mind. My hands shook as the words of my promise to keep him from harm rung in my head.

I grabbed it.

Dashing through the house, I detoured into the living room. I knew what I wanted. Adrian's cell phone and the second pistol. I stashed them into my duffle bag along with the gun I'd picked up from the floor in the back room.

There was no turning back now. No retreat. I would fight this killer on all fronts.

I ran barefoot up the stairs, ripping the light summer clothes from my body. I grabbed black jeans and an ebony sweater from my closet. Hiking boots lay in the corner, still in their original box. I snatched them and pulled on thick socks, then laced up the boots over my ankles. I pulled my hair into a ponytail and tied it out of my way with a leather strap.

I caught my reflection in the dressing table mirror. Who did I think I was? Lara Croft? Not likely. But I was all I had.

I grabbed the duffle bag and ran down the stairs. The best place to start magically tracking was the last place the person in question was seen, in order to tap into the remaining energy. I turned down the hall and pushed through both kitchens until I reached my goal. The back door still swung wildly in the wind, slamming against the wall with a bizarre tempo.

Stepping closer to the doorway, I sensed the electrical buzz of the protective shield I'd cast around the house. Ragged energy danced around a gaping hole punched through it. The puncture throbbed like a fresh cut on skin. I smoothed the edges with my hands, chanting softly. Immediately, the energy calmed.

I closed my eyes and took three deep breaths as I opened my inner vision. Within a few moments, images formed. I could see Adrian, his pistol raised as he spied the open door. He approached cautiously, his eyes wide in the darkness.

"Freeze." *He pointed the pistol at something outside the door.*

"Do it and I'll slice her throat." A voice, steeped in venom.

Adrian lifted his hands, still holding the gun. "Let her go, man. You've already done enough. Don't add to it. Let's talk."

"Don't give me that 'good cop' crap, Burke. Put the gun down or I'll spear her like a pig."

A woman cried out, then the sound choked off.

Adrian lowered the gun, never shifting his gaze from the assailant. "Just keep calm, all right? Let me talk to you."

Silence. Then the voice laughed. "I have a better idea. How about a deal? You come with me, and then I let her go."

I sensed the struggle in Adrian as he considered the request. I knew before he spoke which one he'd make. With another person in danger, it was the only one he could live with.

"Deal."

He walked through the doorway. The protective spell shattered as he passed through the portal, away from the influence of the amulets. Into the path of the killer.

The images stopped. I cursed with frustration. I hadn't seen enough to figure out where they'd gone, but it was enough information to know what I faced. I stepped over the threshold, then closed the door and restored the seal. Only I had the power to break or open the shield from the outside. The house would be secure.

I turned away, guilt piercing me. Why had I worked so hard to forget what I'd learned in childhood? I thought of all the times I could have used the contents of Granny's cedar chest in order to help others, to bring comfort and aid. Maybe even divert the path of a murderer. But I hadn't. In fact, the notion hadn't even crossed my mind until now.

Our natural psychic gifts were one thing. Those were part and parcel of being a MacPherson, and I'd always been proud of them. But I'd made it my goal in my teenage years to deny, avoid, and reject the magical arts, ever since the fiasco with Jake. I'd stood beside Granny when she'd created the original amulets and laughed, calling them "silly hocus-pocus". I thought rejecting magic made me a better person than she, more evolved, more modern. I hung my head for a moment, shamed by the disdainful reasoning of my youth.

My stomach tightened as I thought of every time my mind wandered to something juvenile and trivial while Granny imparted the mysteries of the arts to me. I'd never even read the Book of Secrets. I'd tossed it into the chest along with her other things and locked the lid tight. Now I was paying for my ignorance. I'd allowed events to shape me instead of taking the reins when they were offered. Now the man I loved was missing, in the clutches of a supernaturally driven killer.

A wave of panic lifted over me, threatening to drown me. Sean. The raven-haired tourist. Jake. Mitch. I couldn't let the same thing happen to Adrian. I had to save him.

The path away from the house split into two directions. I didn't know which one to choose. I reached out with my gifts, to pick up any remaining energy. The trail was cold. Even Granny's tools couldn't help now. I needed a magical bloodhound.

I looked into the night sky and did the only thing I could do. I called out to the ancestors. "Help me, Great Cailleach. I know I've failed you in so many ways. But I'm ready to be who I am. I embrace my destiny. Help me save Adrian. Please! Guide me, Great Winter Crone of the Mountain. Show me the way."

The stars twinkled above my head, cold and unheeding. I sighed, bitter desperation thick in my mouth. Then a dim light began to shimmer in front of me, like a flame without a candle. It grew brighter, until at last it bounced lightly in the air in front of my face.

A gift from the Cailleach.

"Thank you," I cried out into the darkness.

The light bobbled a bit in the air, then began to drift down the path to my right. I followed.

Magical bloodhound, on the hunt.

*****

I walked for what seemed like an eternity. The stiff new hiking boots dug into my toes, but I ignored the pain and kept going. The light flickered ahead of me like a beacon, leading me to the shoreline. I tracked behind it, shifting the duffle bag onto the opposite shoulder. At least I'd left the Book of Secrets at home. The bag was beginning to weigh more by the second.

Adrian's cell phone rang in my pants pocket, vibrating against my skin. I pulled it out and punched the button.

"Hello?" My voice sounded muffled by the roar of the sea. Would the caller even hear me?

"Burke? That you?"

I recognized the voice. Lieutenant Andrews. Time to come clean.

"Lieutenant? It's Selene MacPherson. Something's happened to Adrian. He's missing. I think the killer may have him. I'm at McAllister Beach, following the trail. I need you to send a team of your men out here as fast as you can."

"Burke, missing? Stay out of it. I'm getting a group of my men together now to head your direction. Stay where you are, MacPherson. You have to-"

"What? I can't hear you." I drew the phone away

from my face and watched as the battery died. Great. Three cheers for technology. I stuck the useless device back into my pocket. I'd done what I could in the everyday sense. The rest was up to me.

The light glowed a bit brighter, as if changing course and needing me to pay attention.

"Lead on," I called out.

Over the rise of a tall sand dune, the beach turned into a mixture of sea grass, small hills and pines. I climbed as fast as I could, trying to keep the blob of light in my sight. It was traveling too fast now. I couldn't keep up.

"Wait!" I cried, grabbing a thick clump of grass as I pulled myself up a hill. The illumined ball danced above my head, as if set on pause. I cleared the rise, my muscles screaming for relief. Then I saw it.

In the distance, an abandoned beach house stood. The last few hurricanes that swept through the area had turned this part of the terrain into pine mulch at least three times in a row. The tall, two-story house in front of me appeared to have borne the brunt of the impact. It leaned to the left at least twenty degrees. Reminded me of the Leaning Tower of Pisa. Shutters hung from their hinges, one of them insistently flapping in the wind. The original color of the house was indiscernible. Storms and sand had blasted the paint away, leaving raw, naked wood exposed. Tall grass surrounded the house, bending beneath the wind in the gray moonlight. It was right out of a Hollywood horror movie.

A flash of light moved across one of the broken windows. I knew I'd found my destination.

I wasn't surprised by the murderer's choice of

hideout. This is what he'd wanted. His flair for the dramatic had been evident with each murder. He wanted each of us to suffer in our own way, for as long as possible. At least until he obtained his ultimate goal.

I stood and faced the house, my boots filled with sand. I shouldn't go inside. Lieutenant Andrews and his men were on their way. It was safer, smarter to wait for them.

But Adrian had been right, that night on my doorstep. Sometimes the smart thing isn't what we ought to do. I'd tried to think my way out of almost every event in my life the past few years. It was time to let my inner spirit do the talking.

My spirit said, "Go."

I pulled Adrian's pistol from the duffle bag, the cold, silver barrel shimmering in my hand. I stuck a second gun into the rear waistband of my jeans. Then I roped Granny's amethyst amulet around my neck.

I went.

I didn't have to worry about the front door emitting the stereotypical creak as I opened it. Only a portion of the door remained. I stepped around the jagged edge of the wood, careful to keep my clothes from catching. Then I dragged the duffle bag inside. Adrian's gun weighed heavy in my hand. I knew it was loaded, but beyond that, I was clueless how to use it. I had only three thoughts. *Point, shoot, and don't miss.*

I crept across the warped floor of the living room as it rolled beneath my feet like a miniature sea. Water from the storms had turned the once beautiful tiled floor into a disaster. I paused, holding my breath. What if I stepped on a spot too weak to hold my weight and I fell through? I forced myself to breathe and used my foot to measure the strength of the wood frame beneath me.

I lifted the duffle bag onto my left shoulder, keeping my right arm free. I cleared the main room and peered around the corner of the central hallway. The sea roared outside, an incessant rumble against my eardrums. There were no other sounds. Not yet.

A cold bead of sweat tricked downs my right temple. I brushed it away and ground my teeth against the fear digging into my spine. I shouldn't have done this. I should have waited for the police. I was only one person.

"I won't tell anyone. You can still get away. Just let us go!" A woman's wail, high and thin, sounded from the end of the hallway.

I moved from the shadows into the corridor. Then I lifted the gun.

"Shut up," a voice answered. I heard the sound of a fist striking delicate skin. Then a crude laugh.

"What's the matter? You liked it rough the other night." More laughter.

"Leave her alone."

My breath caught. Adrian.

"Shut up, Burke. I'll get to you. In fact, you'll be last. The star of the show."

I crept to the door where the voices originated. Keeping to the shadows, I did my best to get a look at what awaited me.

A long, narrow room faced the pines behind the house. Large picture windows stood bare along the walls, each with long shards of glass missing. The wind stirred the room from different directions as the scattered light of the moon cast odd shadows.

Adrian's side was toward me as he glared at the killer. Gratitude flooded me at the sight of him alive. A rivulet of blood ran down one side of his face, but I couldn't see any other injuries. His hands and feet were bound, tied to the wooden chair where he sat. His bare chest heaved as the killer walked into my line of vision.

He was dressed in a pair of jeans and a thick sweater, a wool cap pulled over his head. He walked to Adrian, his face obscured by the shadows. In his hand was a knife, missing part of its shank.

My hand tightened around the gun.

The killer stood straight, looking out the window into the distance. Then he turned his head to the side and chuckled. "Is that you, Selene? I knew you'd come."

My blood froze at his words. I'd made no sound. How had he known?

"Let me see you, darling. I can feel you when you're near."

"Run!" Adrian cried out.

The killer swung the knife toward him, holding it just under his chin.

"Show yourself, Selene, or your playmate will get it right now."

I stepped from the doorway, holding the gun ready. The voice of the killer sounded familiar, even in his anger, but the moment his gaze touched me, I knew.

He smiled, his eyes bright. "There you are. The prettiest girl in town."

Richard Swann.

The moonlight lit his perfect, chiseled face, the sweep of blonde hair across his forehead. The man I'd seen every day in my restaurant. I'd laughed and joked with him as we'd shared stories. I'd even desired him, at least physically. The man I'd thought of as harmless.

The man to whom I'd willingly introduced my best friend. I could see her behind him, tied to a chair in the same way as Adrian. Janell's blonde curls hung over her face as her head lolled back and forth. She lifted her gaze to me. One eye was swollen nearly shut.

"Selene!" she cried. "I didn't know."

"Neither did I, 'Nell." I circled slowly toward the picture windows, the gun trained on Richard. "Put down the knife," I ordered.

He lifted it a little higher as a small trickle of blood began to run under Adrian's chin. "I don't think so. Put down the gun, or I'll have to start the finale of the show early."

The pinch of metal behind my back reminded me that I had a second option at my disposal. Richard lifted the knife a bit higher. Adrian bit back a groan of pain.

"If I put down the gun, will you let Adrian and Janell go?"

He laughed. "Probably not. But I might refrain from killing them for a while."

"Not good enough."

"Too bad. I appear to be holding all the cards. Tarot, if you prefer." He lifted Adrian's chin with the blade. "The King of Cups here." Then he jerked his head toward Janell. "The Queen of Wands over there." He looked at me and smiled. The deranged entity inside glowed in his eyes.

I had to stall for time. *Where are you, Andrews?"* Why are you doing this, Richard?" I lowered the gun a few inches, to give him the impression I'd softened.

The ploy worked. He pulled the blade away from Adrian's neck and faced me.

Adrian shook his head at me, his expression frantic as he silently urged me to flee. It took all my courage to pull my gaze away from him and look at Richard.

"Why? Aren't you happy to write me off as a simple madman? Chief Burke certainly was." He laughed bitterly, then glanced at Janell. "She thought I was the answer to her prayers, didn't you, baby? Watch out for what you wish for. You might get it."

He swung his face toward me. "But you. You want to know why, don't you? You want to understand. That's like you, Selene. I knew it from the moment I saw you. You're not like them. You're like Alice. She always saw the good in me." His face fell, lost in remembrance.

I sensed the hold of the entity lessen as the wild gleam in his eyes receded slightly. Was this the key to defeating it?

I swallowed, then took a deep breath and focused on visualizing Richard in a ball of soft, white light. Gentle, calm, soothing. "Tell me about Alice."

He sighed in response. "Beautiful. Loving. My everything. We married too young. I was too stupid to know what I had. I chased her away. She left, took the light of my life with her. My Katie."

"Katie?"

"Our daughter. My little one. She looked just like Alice. She cried when Alice took her away. She kept calling for me, 'Daddy, Daddy.'" Richard's voice trembled. "Alice cried, too. I tried to get her back, but she wouldn't come. She moved far away, said she didn't need me anymore. But she did. I know she did."

A flare of anger burst through him, shattering the pale ball of light I'd constructed. I stepped back, surprised by the power unleashed in him. He glared at me but swung his attention to Adrian.

"Then he killed them."

"What?" My hold on the gun wavered.

Richard walked toward Adrian and caught a fistful of his hair, jerking his head to face him. "He killed them. Used his car as a weapon. The coroner told me Katie died instantly. Alice's neck broke. They died on the street, like little dolls left out in the rain. All alone, without me."

Richard's voice broke, then he shoved Adrian's chair with his foot, toppling it backward to lean against the wall.

"I lost my wife, too." Adrian's legs dangling from the upturned chair. "It was an accident. Our cars skidded on ice. Nothing could have changed it."

Richard stood over him, fingering the knife. "That's where you're wrong. I can change it. I can make it end up the way it should have."

"What are you saying?" I lifted the gun higher and leveled it on him.

"By killing him, now."

"No!" I screamed. I pulled the trigger, praying

for my aim to strike true.

The bullet hit the wall over Richard's head. I was off by at least a foot.

Richard lunged at me and grabbed my arm, bashing my hand against the window glass behind me. The leftover pane shattered, cutting my skin. The gun flew out the open window. Blood gushed from my wound.

He hesitated at the sight. "Why do you make me hurt you, Selene? I'm trying to protect you from him, don't you see? I can't let him hurt you, I can't let him take you away from me the way he did with Alice."

He pushed me to the ground and pulled out a handkerchief from his pocket. He bound my hand, then lifted me roughly to my feet. I fought him, digging my nails into his face.

He responded by hitting me so hard, everything went gray. My knees went out from under me. He cradled my body next to his as my head rolled back.

"Don't fight me, love. It's for the best. Once I kill him, once we dump Janell, we can be together. I'll make it right this time. I promise."

I shoved against his chest, struggling to regain my wits. He dragged me toward Adrian and set me beside the chair.

"It's time, Burke." Richard lifted the knife. "I hope you appreciated the little four-act play I created with my blade. Did you like it?"

Adrian lifted his head, his gaze defiant. "Forget it, Swann. Why? Why kill all the others when all you wanted was me?"

"You don't get it, do you? I wanted you to feel death coming. I wanted you to feel as helpless and useless as I did, a thousand miles away when you killed my family. I wanted you to watch and know that no matter what you did, they were all going to die. It was fun, killing them. I picked each man individually, because they looked like you. Call it target practice."

He laughed again, a sound so eerie and terrifying that I wasn't sure how much of Richard still remained human.

Adrian pressed further. "Why the fingers?"

"Did you like that touch? Really threw the cops off with that one. They were so busy trying to figure out some kind of exotic message to it. It was simple. I took two new trophies for every kill. One for Alice. One for Katie."

I shivered at his next words.

"I'll take all ten of yours. After you're dead."

That was it. I pushed from my seated position, hitting him at the knees. The surprise move knocked him off balance. He fell hard onto the floor. I grappled for the gun at my back and pulled it out.

He was faster. He grabbed my hand and rolled with me, pinning me under him. His masculine strength, coupled with the power of the entity, crushed the bones in my hand until I released the weapon. He took the pistol, stuffing it in his pants.

"I do love that about you, Selene. You never give up." He laughed again. His hips ground into my flesh with a dark promise. "I can't wait to see what all that fire is like under more pleasurable circumstances."

"You'll never know, you bastard." I screamed, struggling to throw him off me. If I was going to die, it wouldn't be like this.

I could hear Janell crying as we struggled on the floor. Adrian screamed at him to let me go, his voice cracking with pain.

The entity's hold on Richard increased as we fought. He rose over me and took hold of my throat, choking off the air from my lungs. I gasped, clawing at his arms.

A rich purple glow began to emanate from my chest. It lifted toward Richard's face, white light mixing with the purple. He screamed when the light touched his skin, then he fell backward.

Grandmother's amulet.

My lungs burned like fire as air returned. I rolled onto my side, gagging as I fought the urge to vomit.

"So you'd deny me?" Richard yelled as he climbed to his feet. "It doesn't matter. I'll still finish what I came to do." He turned toward Adrian, the knife in his hand high above his head.

Headlights from vehicles flooded the room with light. I rolled over. The hill above the house filled with cars. The silhouetted figures of men scurried over the sea grass, hunting their prey.

"Too late," I choked out. "It's over, Richard."

"Not quite." He slashed the ropes that held Adrian's feet with the knife and dragged him out of the chair and onto the floor. Adrian kicked at him but Richard out stepped, then responded with his own kick to the side of Adrian's head.

Adrian grew still.

Richard looked at me as I struggled to rise. He paused, a look of conflict so deep in his eyes that I thought he might have the strength to pull away from

his inner master.   Then his expression changed.
Darkness overcame him once more.   He dragged
Adrian out of the room.

*****

"Janell, come on, we've got to follow him."   I
pulled at Janell's ropes until they slipped free.

She grasped my sweater frantically, her eyes
bright with hysteria. "He's going to kill us! Kill us!" I
knew she couldn't hear me.

I shook her, trying to bring her back. "No, not if
we stop him now."

She dissolved into tears. I hugged her to my
breast. I had to do this alone.

"Stay here," I commanded, looking into her eyes.
"Tell the police what happened.   Tell them I went
after them."

I turned from her, then grabbed the abandoned
duffle bag in the corner of the room. With the entity
in charge of Richard, only the way of the ancients had
a chance against him.

I ran down the stairs, my lungs tight. I knew it
would take the police at least ten minutes to work
their way to the beach house in the darkness. I could
wait for them. But ten minutes was more than Adrian
had to spare.

The darkness overwhelmed me. Clouds rolled in,
obscuring the moon.

I screamed into the night. "Show me the way,
Great Cailleach."

The little light that led me to the house suddenly
appeared in front of my nose. Then it flew to the left.
I shifted the bag higher on my shoulder and ran after

it.

"Hold on, Adrian." I sent him the full force of my love.

"Don't follow, Selene."

I paused for a split second as the sound of his voice rung in my head. The odd, inner connection we'd experienced at the second murder scene hadn't been a fluke. It was real. It was now. "Don't tell me what to do. Fight, Adrian. I'm coming."

I ran faster as my small, luminous guide led me into the pines.

Chapter Fourteen

Pine needles swept my face as I dove into the woods. I ignored the sharp stings and bent low beneath the branches, scrambling to keep up with the advancing light. The stakes were higher now. Richard wasn't armed with just a knife. He had a gun. Fully loaded.

And I had a knapsack full of stones and herbs.

My confidence sank like an anchor at the thought. What good were these against a bullet? Thanks to my years of avoidance, I barely remembered how to use most of Granny's magical belongings. The only thing on my side was my innate understanding of the Otherworld that lay beyond this one. I hoped that was enough.

The tiny pinpoint of light slowed its forward motion, then hovered for a moment before it lifted into the trees and disappeared. Wherever Adrian and Richard had fled, they couldn't be far now.

To my left was a large crevice in the hillside, dug out by the lash of one too many storms. I headed for it. It would be my choice, if I were Richard. I picked my way carefully over the thick mounds of dirt, sand, and grass, stopping at every third pine tree to listen for any clues to Adrian's location. So far, the only sound was the distant murmur of the sea behind me.

Maybe I'd misunderstood the disappearance of the light. Did the lifting mean for me to keep going in the same direction, straight ahead? If so, I was off course and wasting precious time. I jerked my head around, cursing as I looked in the other direction. I backed up, intent on retracing my steps.

"Leaving so soon?" An arm shot out from behind me and wrapped around my neck. Richard. He pulled me tight against him, my body bent backward over the duffle bag. The edge of the blade inside the bag nudged against my spine. Why hadn't I thought to take it out? My confidence evaporated. Carelessness would be my death.

I reached up and pulled at his arm as he dragged me over the grass. "Give it up, Richard," I begged. "The state police are here. They're following me. You won't get away."

He chuckled against my ear. "I think I will. I've enjoyed my little vacation in Fort Bedford. Spent a lot of time in these woods, exploring, preparing. Come and see."

He showed me his knife, lifting it in front of my face.

"But first, we need to get rid of this." He sliced through the leather cord that bound Granny's amulet to my neck. The stone dropped to the earth with a soft thud. The sound brought a fresh edge of fear to my heart. I was bare of protection now. Exposed.

He walked, dragging me backward with the strength of two men. My feet struggled to keep my body upright as I stumbled over grass mounds and debris. I held onto his arm to keep my head up and prevent my windpipe from collapse.

I was abruptly thrown onto the ground, the duffle bag flying away from me. I looked up at Richard as I gasped for breath.

"Selene." A weak voice came from the corner of the small cave carved out of the hillside.

Adrian. His chest showed white in the darkness. He was on his back, blood pouring from a knife wound in his side. I crawled to him, frantic. "Adrian! Oh, God, oh, God." I held my hands over the wound, pressing it. Hot fluid poured through my fingers. He was going to bleed to death, right before my eyes.

"How touching." Richard stood over us. "Get back, Selene. I want to see the culmination of my work."

"Go to hell!" I screamed, launching myself at him. He stepped aside, laughing as I fell hard, hitting my head against the wall of the earthen cave.

"I've lived in hell, ever since the accident. Now he'll join me."

Richard knelt down, dangling the knife over Adrian's chest. "How's it feel, to bleed away and see everything you have go with you? You took it all from me. I didn't even get to be there when Alice died. You got to be with your wife until the end. You didn't deserve that privilege. I did."

He made a sound in his throat, flicking the knife upward in his palm. "I hated you for killing Alice. For taking my baby, Katie. But most of all, I hated you because you lived. Your face, all over the newspapers when you got out of the hospital. Brave, courageous Adrian Burke. The lone survivor. The hero. Tried to save his wife from death. What about my wife, Burke? What about mine!"

Richard plunged the knife. Adrian moved, trying to deflect. The blade struck his shoulder, sinking deep. He screamed as Richard crowed in triumph.

I scrambled to the lost duffle bag, thrusting it open and digging for Grandmother's blade. She'd told me as a child to never to use it to draw blood, only to part and direct energy.

I was going to part energy, all right. I was going to part the evil entity from this world.

My fingers grasped the handle of the blade. I pulled hard. It burst free from the bag with a flash of silvery fire. I stumbled to my feet and ran toward Richard as he knelt over Adrian's prone form. Then I stuck the blade into his back as hard as I could.

Richard's body shot straight up as the knife struck home. He howled with an unearthly scream, stumbled a few steps away, and fell forward on his face.

I stood over him, my hand dripping with Adrian's blood. With Richard's blood. A flush of nausea shot up from my stomach as tears came to my eyes.

"No." Adrian moaned, capturing my attention.

I flew to his side. "Adrian. Oh thank God, you're still alive." I cradled his head in my hands. "Andrews is on the way. Hang on."

I ran to the duffle bag, pulling out the shirt he'd stripped from his body earlier that night. I hadn't known why I'd grabbed it. I only knew that I'd wanted something that belonged to him, like a talisman of his love. Now I knew the reason why I'd been led to bring it. I tore the shirt in two as best I could, pressing both knife wounds with the cloth to staunch the blood.

His eyes rolled back in his head, his lashes fluttering shut. I pushed harder on the cloths. The blood soaked through.

"No!" I cried. "Don't die, Adrian. Stay with me.

I love you. Please don't leave me. You said you wouldn't leave me alone." My tears fell on the hard planes of his chest, clinging to the light dusting of wiry black hair.

"MacPherson!"

I lifted my head, my vision clouded with tears.

Lieutenant Andrews. He'd found us.

"Here!" I screamed. "Over here!"

Within moments, I was surrounded by State Police. They went into swift action. One of them had a medical kit. He went to work on Adrian as other men scattered over the area, their police radios squawking as they called for reinforcement.

I grabbed Andrews' arm. "It was Richard Swann. The tourist, the one who hung out at my restaurant."

He nodded. "We know. Miss Wilson told us the whole story."

"Is Janell all right?"

He shrugged as he motioned to some of his men. "A little beat up, but okay otherwise. She told us what you did, MacPherson. Stupid, but brave."

I ignored his comment. "Thanks. Richard's body. It's over there."

Andrews looked at me, his brow furrowed. "What body?"

"Richard Swann. I stabbed him in the back. He's dead. Right over.." I pointed to where he'd had fallen. "There."

Nothing. The cave was empty.

The Lieutenant cocked his head. "You say you stabbed him? Are you sure?"

I pushed the hair out of my face, my mind reeling. "Of course I'm sure. I used my Grandmother's knife.

Where is he?"

Andrews walked to where I'd pointed and knelt down. Then he turned to me.

"Is this the blade?"

I walked to his side. Grandmother's blade, without a hint of blood, lay in his hands. It didn't make sense.

"Maybe you missed and thought you hit him. Don't worry. We'll catch him. You can rely on that. You'll get this back when the investigation is over." Andrews rose to his feet, pulling out an evidence bag.

"Yes." I absently stared at the knife. I'd seen it plunge into Richard's back. I'd felt the impact, smelled the stench of fresh blood as it hit the air. But he was gone. Like a dream.

Or a nightmare.

*****

Adrian's eyes opened. He blinked a few times at a shaft of light from the hospital hallway and turned his head toward me.

I breathed a sigh of relief and took his hand. "Hi."

"Hi." A wan smile lifted the corner of his lips.

"How are you feeling?"

A little moan of pain escaped him as he shifted in the bed. "Like I got stabbed a couple of times. What about you? You all right?"

"I am, now that you're awake." I lifted my hand to brush his thick, black hair away from his brow. Away from the bandages covering the wounds to the head he'd received as Richard's captive. The nurses had cleaned and bandaged my hand as well.

Thankfully the cut from the broken window wasn't as bad as I'd originally thought.

What a pair we were. White-gauzed mummies in the making. I swallowed back tears and tried to smile for him.

He gave my hand a squeeze. "Don't ever do that again, Selene."

"Do what?"

"Try and get yourself killed. That's my line of work." His grimaced as another wave of pain hit him. Then he settled back onto the pillow.

"Tell you what." I dropped a light kiss on his forehead. "You quit that line of work, and I will, too."

He smiled, his eyes closing as the drugs took hold again. "Deal." His eyes opened briefly and he looked at me with alarm. "Swann?"

"No longer a problem." What sense was there in telling him the truth?

He sighed in relief and slipped into slumber. I pressed another shaky kiss to his brow before I left the room.

Andrews waited for me. We stepped back against the wall as two nurses rushed past us.

"He's going to make it." Andrews whipped out a cigarette.

I pointed to the "No Smoking" sign posted directly in front of us.

He shrugged and put the unlit stick back into his jacket pocket. "He's a lucky guy."

"Absolutely." I leaned against the wall, closing my eyes for a moment.

"What about you? You want police protection at your house until Swann is captured?"

I'd learned my lesson. No more going it alone. I looked up at Andrews and nodded. "I'd appreciate that."

"I'll have a man posted there within the hour."

"Thank you, Lieutenant." I reached up and gave his cheek a kiss.

He grinned like a sheepish schoolboy. "Yeah, well, no problem. Hey, if I ever need a psychic on a case again, can I call you?"

I walked down the hall toward the elevator. Then I turned and looked at Andrews and nodded. "I'm your woman."

*****

I didn't think there could ever be anything more extraordinary than the feeling I had when I returned home. The house, its energy, its welcome, reached out to embrace me as I walked up the front steps. I paused for a moment, eyeing the wooden swing on the porch as it moved gently with the morning breeze. Things had changed for Adrian and me on that swing, despite how the night had ended. He'd trusted me. And I'd opened up to a man, for the first time in years.

I glanced at the empty parking lot at the west side of the House. For the first time in five years, Mimosas and Magnolias had failed to open for business. I wasn't sure when I'd have the energy to dish out culinary delight again. Weariness weighed heavy on my body as I put the key in the door. It would be so good to go to bed, to sleep, and hopefully not to dream. I didn't want to see the things I'd seen the past week, ever again.

I turned the key, pushed the door open, and walked inside. In that second, I realized my mistake.

Too late.

The impact of Richard's body from behind shoved me at least six feet across the foyer. I flew forward, landing on the stretch of carpet leading to the main staircase.

"Forgot to open the shield, bitch." He slammed the door behind him. "You walked right through it. Only you could break it from the outside. Thanks for taking care of that for me."

I rolled onto my back and glared at him, panicked when I realized I'd left the duffle bag in the car.

Richard circled me, smiling as he drew the knife from his coat pocket.

I pushed myself away from him on my back. "I killed you. How can you still be alive?"

"You killed what used to be Richard. But not me."

The thing that stood before me grinned with victory. It was Richard's body, but his human soul had fled. The evil had taken over his form. It ruled completely.

I backed further away, frantic for escape. The entity advanced toward me slowly, taking its time the way a cat plays with a mouse. Until the mouse becomes dinner.

My back hit the staircase. I turned and darted up the stairs on my hands and knees, until at last I was able to regain my footing.

"You might as well not run, Selene. I'm going to kill you anyway." He put a foot on the stairs and followed me.

I ran down the hallway to my room, then shut the door and pushed the lock. I shoved the chest of drawers in front of it.

I cringed at the ridiculousness of what I'd done. A chest of drawers full of lingerie? That wouldn't hold him off for long. Stupid, stupid. I'd trapped myself in an upstairs bedroom with no mode of escape. I was famous for making fun of characters in horror films that acted this way.

His footsteps sounded on the hallway floor. I moved away from the door. Pressing my back against the wall, I dredged through my mind for a solution. Why had I left the duffle bag in the car? Why?

"You never did pay attention to that lesson."

I jerked my head to the right, straining to hear.

"Granny?"

Her sweet laughter filled my head. "Stubborn girl, always. But I didn't mind. I knew that stubbornness would turn into strength one day."

The doorknob rattled briefly. Then the entity began to pound on the door. The impact of his body sounded like a sledgehammer.

My heart rose to my mouth as I held back the urge to scream. "Help me, Granny. I'm unarmed. I don't have any of the things you left me. I'm defenseless."

"Are you?"

I did scream then, in terror and frustration. "I don't have time for questions now. Tell me!"

"You always thought my tools were worthless. But you never caught on to the word 'tool'. They are only that, Selene. They are beneficial helps, aids. They are not the magic. You are."

"Me?"

"Who are the friends of the MacPhersons? Who waits for the sound of our invitation?"

The old rhyme we used to chant together when I was a child began to echo in my head.

Fires burning bright at night,
Wind blows strong at morning light,
Earth rolls rich beneath our feet,
Waters rise to pleadings sweet.
All will come and attend us strong
When The MacPherson calls them with a song.

The ancient pine wood splintered with the last flurry of blows, breaking away from the lock. The chest of drawers squeaked against the bare floor as the door opened.

I turned to face my attacker and lifted my arms high. Immediately a ray of clear, bright light shot down through the ceiling and struck the top of my head, filling me with its brilliant power.

The entity in Richard's body smirked as he raised the knife.

"Earthen spirits, hear my cry. Release the fury you hold on high!"

At that instant the earth began to shudder beneath our feet. The house shook as items on my vanity table fell and shattered on the floor.

Richard grabbed at the wall but came up empty-handed. He fell hard onto his back in the hallway, the knife skittering a few feet away.

Strength surged in me, lifting my energy higher. I walked toward the door and pointed my right index finger at Richard. A channel for the elements.

"Wind of the heavens, come to me. Cast him

aside, out toward the sea!"

A mighty blast of air swept through the house, rattling the pictures on the wall and sending any loose papers flying. It was like being inside a wind tunnel. Richard scooted across the floor like a plastic bag left discarded on the street. He grabbed for the railing of the staircase and held on, but the force of the gale was too strong. It whipped around him until at last he tumbled down the stairs, his body flipping wildly.

I followed him, the wind tearing the rest of my hair from the leather tie at my neck until it flew about my head and face like billowing clouds.

Richard's body hit the front door with a dull thud. He rolled onto his stomach and looked up at me, death in his gaze.

"Not that easy!" he screamed. Suddenly the same muddy, noxious cloud I'd seen obscuring him in my visions formed around his body. Then it roiled upwards, like the funnel of a tornado, as Richard pulled to his feet.

Stale, heavy, and sweet, I recognized the smell of it. The scent of decay. Of death.

I lifted my arms and the wind rose, shoving Richard hard against the front door.

He mirrored my actions. The cloud of venomous poison moved my direction.

I did the only thing I could think of. I ducked and headed for the restaurant door. If he wanted to battle, he would do it on my turf.

The natural world.

I ran through both kitchen doors, heading for the back exit, the place where all of this had begun. Flinging open the outer door, I took off over the field behind the house, heading straight for the beach. The place where the Cailleach had spoken. Where Jake had died.

The sound of running footsteps behind me urged me on, faster and harder. I couldn't let him catch me. Elemental allies or not, I knew I couldn't defeat his superior physical strength. The power of my will and the strength of my faith would have to come to my rescue this time. The real magic.

I finally cleared the grass and ran onto the soft sand dunes, cursing as they sucked at my hiking boots and slowed my progress. His hand grazed the edge of my shoulder. I screamed and pushed myself until my feet hit the wet, sturdy shore.

I glanced into the sky and called above the roar of the sea. "Sacred Fire, Spirit of Power. Send your flame to save this hour!"

Suddenly the gentle, puffy white cloud huddled just over the edge of the waves boiled into an angry gray. In an instant, a hot flash of lightning burst from it, striking the ground at Richard's feet. He screamed and fell as the current traveled through the moisture in the sand and delivered a powerful jolt.

I turned and ran down the edge of the water, trying to make it to the little row of shops down the beach. If I could only reach them, I knew Richard wouldn't follow. It would cost the entity too much to reveal himself that way. I'd be safe, for a time. Until I could formulate a better plan.

I didn't have the courage to look back, to see if he'd risen from the electrical shock. He'd already fooled me once. But I should have looked back. I would have seen it coming, if I had.

A cold, clinging cloud of murky brown drifted beside me, keeping up with my pace. I picked up speed, desperate to outrun it. It overtook me.

I fell to the sand as the first breath from the cloud hit my lungs like sweet, burning tar. I crawled toward the grassy area, away from the beach, but the fog only closed tighter around me, like a macabre blanket from a death-dealing mother.

"Poor Selene." Richard crooned to me as he walked into the cloud. "You make everything so hard. The other victims went without a whimper. Nice, quick, easy death. Why do you always choose to suffer?"

I gazed up at him, my breathing becoming more difficult by the second. He didn't have to use a knife this time. He was going to suffocate me instead. I gasped, choking. "What are you?"

He laughed. "You can call me a force of inspiration. I provoke men to the depths of depravity. I've used this body, but I've been a lot of different men. Richard is small potatoes. But I'll take whatever I can get, to keep in practice." He walked to my side, smiling like a schoolteacher explaining physics. "It's easy, actually. All they have to do is open to me. Once they become willing to do anything to get what they want, they give me an opportunity. The moment they make the choice to embrace their anger, I can take my place inside them."

"Small potatoes?" My brain was beginning to lose the thread of his words. I put a hand to my throat, wheezing for air.

He shrugged. "I've done better. Terrorists are my favorite right now, but so many of them seem to like blowing themselves up. I have to leave before a subject dies, or I die as well. I have to thank you, Selene. You gave me a unique opportunity when you stabbed Richard. I pulled out and watched, you know. Nice work with the knife. While he was still warm, I returned to him. I didn't know I could re-inhabit a host after death. Interesting. Haven't a clue why I never gave it a try before."

He shook his head and shot me a grin, his pearly-white teeth stark against the filthy brown cloud bubbling around us. "But then again, I bore so easily. I enjoy a host who takes his time, spreads his crimes out over a number of years. Serial killers are my most preferred. They know how to enjoy the kill, truly savor it. When a host becomes an artist at his work, I grow stronger."

He stretched his arms in front of him, as if testing the merchandise. "Richard is a good choice for now. I've never been in a host that other people take to heart so quickly. He's so likable, so attractive. Think of the number of women I'll be able to get with this body. What fun. So many rewarding, pleasurable kills."

He smiled at me again, his movie star face masking the darkest evil I'd ever known. I crawled further toward the dunes as he stood admiring his packaging.

My consciousness was fading. I knew my own death was near. But I couldn't let this monster win. I had one more ally on my side.

I lifted my arms one last time. With the final breath in my lungs, I called out. "Queen of the Ocean, Star of the Sea. Take this evil with you and set the world free!"

The tide suddenly pulled away from the shore with such force that it made a sucking sound, like bathwater slipping down a drain. Richard turned, a shocked expression on his face.

The sea built, rising higher and higher, rushing forward with conscious thought. Richard screamed and began to run in my direction, but it was too late. A wave, fifteen feet high, rose over him, the crest white with foam. Then it crashed down, the pound of the surf so strong that it shook the earth beneath me. The toxic mist vanished as Richard's body lifted up and carried out to sea.

The last thing I saw was his Robert Redford blonde hair as it slipped beneath the water.

Epilogue

"A little bit to the right."

"Here?"

Odette cocked her head and took two steps back. "Now it's too high. Bring it down a little."

I blew a lock of hair out of my eyes and lowered the frilly red heart a few inches.

"There. It's perfect."

I pushed a pin into the decoration, fastening it to the wall. "I'm glad you're happy now."

Odette laughed and walked toward her usual table. "You always said your motto was, 'We aim to please!' Well, this is part of it. The place looks great, Selene. A perfect day for the grand opening."

I climbed down the ladder and brushed my hands on my denim skirt. "You're absolutely right."

Outside the window, the cool February breeze swung the three wooden signs I'd hung that morning in front of MacPherson House. The first sign read Mimosas and Magnolias; Southern-style Home Cooking. The second read Southern Skies Art Studio, Janell Wilson, Owner. The third sign was the newest. Selene's Nemeton—All things Herbal, Metaphysical, and Magical. Tarot Readings by appointment. It was a new day for my ancestral home.

For me, too. I had a lot to accomplish as well as anticipate. Adrian was due to return to Fort Bedford at any time. He'd been away on a case for over a week. I'd missed him more than ever. I walked to the window, telling myself that I wasn't watching for his car to drive up. But I knew that wasn't true.

The town council thought better of their decision to fire Adrian, after the murders ended and Richard Swann's body was discovered washed ashore two miles from Raven's Beach. They'd offered him his old job back. He'd turned them down. Instead, he'd formed a private investigative firm with a fellow ex-Northerner and former cop who lived in Mobile. They investigated insurance fraud, tracking suspects more often with a video camera than a drawn pistol. It was less exciting than the work he'd done before, but he said he'd meant it when he'd vowed to start a new life.

Last night on the phone, he'd said he had news for me. He'd refused to give any other details; I'd just have to be patient. That virtue isn't my strong point. Eagerness escalated with every tick of the clock, but I couldn't dwell on the mystery as much as I'd like. I still had a business to run. As of now, I had two.

Strangely enough, the notoriety and publicity from Richard's killing spree didn't keep people away from Fort Bedford. It drew them in droves. It hadn't hurt that an author had penned a book about the killings and the work of Lieutenant Andrews, Adrian, and me. She'd gotten some of the story right. But no one knew the whole truth, outside the family. It would remain that way.

Adrian and I became minor celebrities. For about fifteen minutes. Then the usual routine of daily life returned. However, the town itself had changed. The horrors we'd endured pulled us together. We came out of the fear-driven mindset that had ruled us for too long and began to love each other a little bit more.

A portion of that newly minted affection found its

way to me, just as I am. Even Arnold James and I worked past our differences and turned over a new leaf in order to live in peace. Who would have thought it possible?

Most of all, I'd learned to give love and forgiveness to the one person I'd denied it most. Myself. I no longer tried to fit into a mold cast by others. A big change, and a welcome one.

As for the entity, my hopes hung on the idea that the wave surprised him before he could transition out of the body. For the sake of the world, I hoped we'd seen the last of him.

I climbed up the ladder again. The heart still needed adjustment. It was too high on the left, despite Odette's help. I'd never decorated the restaurant for Valentine's Day before. I guess I'd never felt part of the "lover's holiday". I did this year. Adrian was the cause.

In the months since Richard Swann's death, I'd nursed him back to health. As his body healed, his heart and spirit did the same. I'd made sure of that. What I didn't expect was how much healing he would bring me. I couldn't imagine life without him. His smile, his jokes, the way he brought out the best in everyone. He had faith in me. Not just magically, which surprised us both, but in every respect. I'd never known anyone with the kind of strength and confidence he possessed, yet he touched me with such tenderness and devotion. He gave all of himself. He'd shown my girls what a real man could be. He'd eventually won them over with his patience and care—even Steph. He'd helped her see beyond her father's abandonment and into the hope for a better future.

I loved him. More than I thought possible. Yet despite it all, I held back a part of myself. I continued to protect the innermost core of my heart. I didn't know if I had it in me anymore, to bare that most vulnerable place to the touch of another. At times I wondered if I would ever be completely whole again. Maybe that just wasn't in the cards.

"I'd sure like to get my hands under that skirt."

I looked over my shoulder and smiled as Adrian's voice echoed inside my head.

"You're lucky no one can hear you but me when you do that. You might scandalize the town."

Adrian grinned, the corner of his mouth lifting. "I don't think there's anything we could do that could scandalize this town. We've done it all. The locals are immune."

I turned on the ladder and reached for him. He stepped forward and took me in his arms, then spun me around as he buried his face in my hair.

He set me on my feet and I cuddled closer to him, smoothing his shirt beneath my hands. "I'm pretty sure we could still come up with something shocking, if we put our minds to it."

He leaned forward, his lips against my ear. "We'll save that for later. Upstairs."

"Is that the news you had for me?" I looked back at him as I walked away toward the family side of the house. I put an extra swivel in my step. His expression told me I had his full and undivided attention.

"No, that's not the news." He followed me through the second swinging door. It closed behind him. "This is." He stopped in the main foyer of MacPherson House, the light from the stained glass window above the front door casting red, blue, and green around us.

I turned toward him, curious.

Before I could say a word, he dropped to one knee and drew a small, black velvet box from his pocket. He took my hand and cleared his throat nervously. Then, lifting his gaze to meet mine, he took a breath and smiled. "It's Valentine's Day. The day when people are supposed to think about love. But ever since I met you, that's all I've been able to do. Remember how I acted that first day at the Festival? I didn't want to believe that anyone like you could be real. But you are. I love you, Selene. You gave me my life back. Now I want to give it to you."

He opened the box. A glittering, clear diamond ring nestled inside.

"Will you marry me?"

I stared at him, my hands shaking. The ghosts who'd haunted me, the fears that held me back for so many years. I could see them, lingering at the edge of my vision. They existed. Their force was strong. But one look into the ocean of love in Adrian's eyes told me that I could find the power to believe again—with him. I smiled and moved closer.

The ghosts slowly faded from my sight. I wouldn't miss them.

"Yes, I will. I love you, Adrian."

He stood, a huge smile on his face as he pulled me into his arms.

"Way to go, Mom."

We broke apart and I glanced toward the

staircase.   Steph and Lissa hung over the upstairs railing, their faces aglow. Izzy and Sarabeth stood in the doorway of Izzy's room. Sarabeth held a tissue to her eye.

I turned to Adrian in apology, but he only laughed and swung an arm wide toward our audience. "How about you guys? You want to marry me, too? It's a package deal, after all."

"We accept." Izzy called out, as Sarabeth's loud, booming laughter echoed down the hall.

Adrian pulled me closer as the whole gang hurried down the stairs toward us. "You never have to cast a love spell on me, honey. I'm yours, for life."

I hugged him tight as the girls leapt to throw their arms around us. I wasn't sure, but I thought I heard the Cailleach's laughter on the wind.

The spiral was complete.

So was I.